VIABLE HOSTAGE

AN EMERALD CITY THRILLER

AUDREY J. COLE

This is a work of fiction. Names, characters, businesses, places, events and incidents are either the products of the author's imagination or used in a fictitious manner. Any resemblance to actual persons, living or dead, or actual events is purely coincidental.

Copyright © 2020 Audrey J. Cole

All rights reserved. No part of this book may be reproduced, scanned, transmitted, or distributed in printed or electronic form without the written permission of the author.

ISBN: 9781089545170

For Elise and Anders, my little ones

CHAPTER ONE

The purr of the yacht's idling engines was the only noise on the calm midnight water of Puget Sound. Until the garbage bag filled with Gretchen's chopped-up body splashed into the sea.

The man returned to the helm of the fifty-foot motor cruiser. He thrust the throttles forward. The vessel vibrated under his feet as the five-hundred-horsepower dual engines roared to life. He cruised forward before making a wide turn back to the city, careful not to run over the bag full of Gretchen's remains as they sank to the bottom.

He had two more bags to dump but thought it best not to sink them all in the same spot.

He sped past the southern tip of Bainbridge Island and veered right toward Elliott Bay. There were faint lights in the distance from the large waterfront estates that bordered the densely wooded island. It would've been a tranquil scene if it weren't for Gretchen's dismembered corpse that filled the remaining trash bags on board.

When his depth finder reached five hundred feet, he threw the boat into neutral. He hurried to the stern where two large black garbage bags rested against the side of the vessel.

He grimaced slightly as he lifted the heavy bag over the edge. Another splash. He looked over the side and waited a moment for it to sink before returning to the helm.

It wasn't Gretchen's death that bothered him. He couldn't believe it had gone so wrong. After all that planning. All that work. For *nothing*.

Gretchen had been the perfect subject. No one even missed her after she disappeared. He'd already been making plans for this kind of research before he'd learned of Gretchen's unwanted pregnancy from a one-night stand.

He had everything in place by the time her fetus got close to viability. Gretchen's kidnapping had gone to a T. His research was about to begin. Until he screwed everything up.

He slammed the throttles into full speed. When he reached the north end of Bainbridge, he eased up on the power. The yacht idled halfway between the island and downtown Seattle before he killed the engines. He moved to the back of the boat. Looking at the dark water that surrounded him, he thought of the two bags containing Gretchen's remains already lying on the floor of the Sound.

He lifted the remaining bag and swung it over the side. He stared at the water's surface as his last three months of work and planning sank to the bottom. A ferry horn blared into the midnight silence, and he jumped at the sound.

He cocked his head and saw that he had drifted into the direct path of the Bainbridge ferry. The large vessel looked less than a hundred feet away. The ferry lights nearly blinded him.

The ferry sounded its second warning, which muted the string of expletives that came out of the man's mouth. He

VIABLE HOSTAGE

ran to the helm and pushed the throttles forward. Nothing happened. The man swore, remembering he'd turned off the engines. He pressed the ignition starter, but the yacht remained quiet.

The ferry blared its horn another time, now less than fifty feet away. The man spun around to see the ferry cutting to the left to move out of his path. The man pulled the throttles back to neutral and pushed the starter again. The engines hummed. The man shoved the throttles forward. He sped away, nearly clipping the ferry's starboard side as it sounded its horn a final time.

The man slammed his fist against the side of the boat. The whole point of dumping the body at midnight was to avoid being seen. Good thing he'd weighted down the bags.

His heart gradually stopped racing as he cruised toward the Ballard Locks just north of the city that would lead him back to Lake Union. He looked around at the Sound's calm waters, thinking of Gretchen's remains down there.

There was only one thing left to do. He'd have to find another pregnant woman that no one would miss. And start over.

CHAPTER TWO
Four Months Later

"Whose idea was it to walk? My feet are killing me."

Malorie smiled at her roommate. She was always overdramatizing things. "We're almost there."

Malorie took a sideways glance at Lani walking awkwardly down the sidewalk in her four-inch heels. They were ridiculous. Especially for the bar they were going to. Harry's was a popular but casual hangout right next to the university campus.

"Is it too late to call an Uber?" Lani asked.

Malorie laughed, not sure if Lani was joking or not. "It's only a block away. Do you need me to carry you? Actually, don't answer that. You're too heavy for me."

Lani feigned a look of shock. "Oh, please."

Although both women were fit, Lani was five inches taller than Malorie, nine if you counted her heels, and weighed about twenty pounds more.

Lani stopped, holding her palms up in the air. "Oh, no. It's raining."

"It's barely sprinkling." Sometimes Malorie wondered if Lani exaggerated for effect, or if she really felt things as strongly as she expressed them.

They reached the bar less than two minutes later. Harry's sign was lit up above the entrance. The establishment was packed as usual for a Saturday night. Harry's was one of the oldest bars in Seattle and almost as old as the university itself. *Since 1889* was proudly displayed in dark blue paint on the front of the building.

When Malorie opened the door to the bar, they were confronted by laughter, shouting, and the clinking of glasses, the sounds from a large group of college students drinking and enjoying themselves. The roommates weaved their way through the other college patrons to get to the bar. They waited five minutes before the bartender approached them. He looked to be a student himself. Maybe even an undergrad.

"What can I get for you two?"

"I'll have a cider," Malorie said.

He nodded and turned to Lani.

"And I'll have a Sprite."

Malorie was proud of her roommate. Despite her wild past, she hadn't seen her take a drink in months. She was a changed person from the one Malorie used to know.

He came back with their drinks a moment later and they looked around for a place to sit. The bar was full, with only one open table in the corner of the room. Malorie followed Lani in a beeline to the table in the crowded space. They set their drinks on the wooden table and took off their coats before sitting down.

"I was going to offer to call an Uber if you're too drunk to walk home. But I guess that won't be a problem," Malorie said with a smirk.

Lani's expression turned serious. "I'm not drinking

tonight. I have other priorities now."

"Yeah, I know." They had three midterms next week. And they both still had hours of studying to do before the weekend was over. "I think that's great. So, what's the award your mom is receiving tomorrow?"

Lani took a drink of her Sprite. "She's getting awarded Best Seattle Doctor by *Pacific Magazine*. They have an event every year to honor the top contenders. She's won it twice before."

"That's amazing."

Lani shrugged her shoulders. "I guess. But, seriously, you don't have to come tomorrow if you don't want to. Especially with our big midterm on Monday. And, the event is actually really boring."

"Of course I want to. I think it's incredible."

"Just don't say I didn't warn you."

Unlike Malorie's parents, Lani's mother and father were both doctors. Malorie knew Lani well enough to know that she resented the fact they expected her and her brother to follow in their footsteps. One night after having too much to drink when they were undergrads, Lani had confided in Malorie that she really wanted to be a detective, not a doctor. But she didn't want to disappoint her mom and dad.

They had never really spoken about it again. Malorie figured that was why Lani was planning to specialize in forensic pathology. Being a medical examiner would be the closest thing to doing what she really wanted to do.

"Don't look," Lani said. "But I think the guys at the table next to us are checking us out."

Malorie glanced at the small table closest to them.

"*I said don't look!*" Lani whispered.

Even from her quick glance, Malorie could tell they were

both hot. They looked to be about their age. Mid-twenties. Probably grad students. One was blond and the other had jet-black hair. The dark-haired one had smiled at Malorie when she looked their way.

"Yeah, I think so too."

Both men stood from their table. "What are you two drinking?" The blond one motioned toward the girls' nearly empty drinks. "We'll get your next round."

Lani's false eyelashes reached her eyebrows as she looked up at him. "A Sprite for me and a cider for her." She smiled flirtatiously.

"You sure you don't want something a little stronger?" he asked.

"I'm sure."

"Got it. A Sprite and a cider."

The two men turned for the bar. Malorie noticed they were both a little unsteady on their feet.

"The one with dark hair is totally into you," Lani said, finishing the last of her Sprite.

"I think they're both a little drunk."

"So?"

"I'll be right back," Malorie said. "I have to pee."

When Malorie returned from the bathroom, their table was empty aside from their drinks, courtesy of their drunk new friends. Malorie hadn't seen Lani on her way back from the restroom. Next to their empty table, their new-found admirers were laughing while they finished their next round of beers.

Malorie turned to them when she got to their table. "Did you guys see where my friend went?"

The dark-haired one looked up at her with large brown eyes. "No. The table was empty when we came back with

VIABLE HOSTAGE

your drinks. We thought you two had bailed."

His words were starting to slur. He clumsily pulled out the chair next to him. "You can sit with us if you want."

Malorie forced a smile. "Thanks, but I think I'll find my friend first."

She looked around the bar. Lani was nowhere in sight. Malorie sat down at their table and pulled out her phone. She texted her roommate. *Where'd you go?*

Malorie's phone rang thirty seconds later. It was Lani.

"Hey, where are you?"

"I'm out front. I just got a call from this guy I've kinda been seeing. He's in the area, and he's going to swing by and pick me up."

"What? You didn't tell me you've been seeing someone. And, you're just going to leave me here?"

"Sorry. It's new."

Malorie stood from their table and walked to the front door of the bar with her roommate still on the phone. She wanted to speak to her face-to-face. *Who was this guy she'd supposedly been seeing?* Ditching her out of the blue seemed odd, even for Lani.

"Plus," Lani added, "you're not really *alone*. That guy that bought our drinks is totally into you."

"Lani—"

"Sorry, Mal. I have to go. He just pulled up. I'll be home later. I shouldn't be late, but, if I am, don't wait up for me."

Malorie pulled her phone away from her ear and saw that Lani had hung up. She swung open the door to the bar and stepped outside. She was alone on the sidewalk. Malorie watched a silver Mercedes pull away from the curb.

Something shiny caught her eye on the ground next to the curb. She recognized the pink rhinestone phone case instantly. She picked Lani's phone up from the wet cement. A photo of the two of them Lani had taken their first year of med school lit up the screen before it prompted for her passcode.

The Mercedes stopped briefly at a red light a block away. The light turned green and the car took off before disappearing around a bend in the road.

Lani had to have been in the Mercedes. She'd been talking to Malorie on her phone seconds before the Mercedes drove away from the bar. Malorie wondered if she should wait in case Lani came back for it. But the car seemed to be long gone, and the earlier drizzle had turned to rain.

She dried Lani's phone screen against her sweater before dropping it into her purse. Lani could be such an airhead sometimes for someone so smart.

She decided not to go back inside the bar. Now, all she wanted was to go home. She turned the street corner to go back to their apartment.

She thought of her roommate as she passed by the undergrad apartment building that Lani had pointed out to her several times. It was where two victims of a famous Northwest serial killer had been last seen alive in the 1970s. Lani found it intriguing, but the building always gave Malorie an eerie feeling.

Malorie regretted not bringing a jacket with a hood. Her hair was soaked by the time she got back to the on-campus apartment she and Lani shared. She used her keycard to unlock the building's main door. As she rode the elevator to the fifth floor, she wondered about the mystery date Lani had ditched her for. She had no idea who it could be. *A student? A doctor?* Not that it mattered. She knew Lani wouldn't keep him around for long. She never did. Not

VIABLE HOSTAGE

since Dante had broken up with her five months ago.

She'd thought Lani had changed. But tonight she'd acted exactly like the person she was before nearly flunking out of med school last spring.

Once inside their apartment, Malorie flicked on the lights and set her purse on the kitchen counter. She'd have to ask Lani about this new guy in the morning. After she'd forgiven her for making her walk home alone in the rain.

CHAPTER THREE

"I can't believe she did this again," Lani's father said, staring at the empty chair next to Malorie.

And neither could she. Malorie sat across the small circular table from him in the banquet hall of the Four Seasons downtown. The Seattle waterfront glimmered in the afternoon sun through the floor-to-ceiling windows behind their table. She glanced at her watch. It was three-thirty, and no one had seen or heard from Lani all day. Lani's mother, Dr. Tatiana Wu, had already received her award, and the *Pacific Magazine* event was winding down.

With Lani missing her phone, Malorie had no way of contacting her. She'd tried to unlock Lani's phone to find out who her mystery date was, but, after trying every password she could think of, she was at a loss. At first, Malorie wondered why Lani didn't have the sense to use her date's phone and let them know she was okay. But then Malorie realized Lani might not have known any of their phone numbers without her contact list. She had sent Lani an email to both her school and personal accounts in case she was able to access them. She hadn't gotten a response. But no one in Lani's family was worried.

Lani's father shook his head in disapproval. "First her brother's college graduation. Now, this."

Lani's younger brother, Tyler, sat to Malorie's right. The last time Lani had done something like this was last May. Lani had gone to a party on a Friday night, gotten drunk and high, and didn't come back to their apartment until Sunday afternoon. She'd been completely MIA for Tyler's college graduation on Saturday.

Tyler had graduated with a pre-med degree just like everyone else in his family. He was now a first-year med student at the University of Elliot Bay, two years behind Lani and Malorie. Malorie had gone to his graduation, expecting Lani to also show up, but she never did. Malorie remembered several awkward family moments just like this as her parents fumed about where she was and why she hadn't shown up to such an important event. Although, that time, her parents were actually concerned something might have happened to her. Unlike now.

After Tyler's graduation, Lani's parents had filed a missing persons report with the Seattle Police. They were beyond livid to learn the next day that their daughter had simply been too drunk and high to come to her brother's graduation. Or let anyone know that she was okay.

That same week, Lani had failed a final exam in one of their classes. She would've flunked out of med school, except that her professor allowed her to retake the final, which was unheard of at the university. Malorie had always wondered if her parents had something to do with the professor's leniency. Not only were they both prominent physicians in the Seattle area, but they were also Elliot Bay University alumni. Lani's father was an adjunct professor at the university, participating in clinical research trials and guest lecturing on occasion.

Lani's boyfriend of four years broke up with her around the same time. Lani never told Malorie the exact reason they'd broken up. Malorie had assumed he got sick of her unpredictability and recklessness.

But Lani had changed. Over the last five months, Malorie had observed her friend become a different person. Lani got serious about school, stopped partying, stopped smoking weed, and only drank on occasion. In fact, it had been months since Malorie had seen Lani have a drink. While Lani continued to be exceedingly flirtatious with almost every hot guy she met, she hadn't dated anyone seriously since her last boyfriend.

Lani's father finished his champagne and turned to his wife. "I'm very proud of you, my love."

Tatiana looked distracted as she returned her husband's gaze. "Thank you, Jian."

"Shall we go?"

She nodded, looking disapprovingly at her daughter's empty seat. "I'm ready."

Tyler attempted to make small talk with Malorie as they followed his parents out of the hotel, but she was too concerned about Lani's whereabouts to engage in much conversation. With her parents in Portland, she'd spent a lot of time, even holidays, with Lani's family since the start of med school. The only family Malorie had in Seattle was her uncle Wade. When they got to the parking garage, Malorie couldn't help but say something.

"I'm worried about Lani."

Lani's family looked at Malorie. None offered a response. Malorie could tell from their faces that they weren't concerned.

"I know she doesn't have her phone, but I think if she were able to call, she would have. She's changed since last spring. I have no idea who she left with last night. I don't think she really knew him either. Maybe she's being held against her will somewhere. Or worse."

Jian and Tyler's expressions were unchanged by what Malorie had said. Tatiana looked at Malorie sympathetically. Her heels were nearly as high as her daughter's the night before, and she leaned over and wrapped her arms around Malorie.

"We're so thankful that Lani has such a wonderful friend like you. Thank you for coming today." She pulled back, leaving her hands on Malorie's shoulders. "We appreciate your concern, but I'm sure, just like last time, Lani is fine. Inconsiderate and irresponsible, but fine. I think it's too soon to worry given her prior behavior. Please let us know when you hear from her."

"I will." Malorie turned and walked down the row to her car. *Why is it so hard for Lani's own family to believe she could change for the good?*

CHAPTER FOUR

At first, Lani only had the strength to open her eyelids halfway. She looked around the room, trying to remember where she was. The room was small. There was a treadmill next to the bed she lay on, which filled the room's remaining space. And the bed wasn't even a twin. Her upper body was inclined 45 degrees with a rail on either side. It was a hospital bed. But her surroundings weren't those of a hospital.

The white walls were bare against the linoleum wood floor. There was a small flat-screen TV on the wall at the end of her bed. A small camera was mounted next to it, pointing in her direction. The door to the room was closed. It matched the white of the walls and had a circular doorknob. Although the room had a feeling of sterility, it seemed more like someone's private home than a medical institution.

She had no recollection of going to sleep. Although the room was unlit, she knew it was daylight from the small amount of sunlight filtering in through the curtains above her head. The sweater she'd worn the night before was gone, replaced by a faded hospital gown.

She took in a deep breath through her nose. She tried to open her mouth, but her lips were stuck together. *Duct tape?* She lifted her hand to pull it away, but it jerked to a stop before it reached her face. Looking down, she saw both her hands were in handcuffs, each attached to the bed's metal rails. As she tilted her head forward, her hair pulled slightly from the duct tape wrapped around the back of her head.

An IV pole hung to her left. A bag of fluid was connected to an IV in her arm. She could tell by the color of the liquid that it was TPN, or total parental nutrition, replacing the need for food by providing her body with all its necessary nutrients.

She tried to scream, but the only noise that escaped the duct tape was a pathetic hum. Her breathing quickened. She tugged her wrists back and forth until her skin was rubbed raw from the cuffs. She gripped the bed rails and pulled with all her might. But she wasn't strong enough to pull them away from the bed. She slid her wrists up and down the rails, but it was no use. The rails were connected to the base of the bed on either side.

A sheet and a thin blanket covered her from the waist down, but she could feel that her ankles were also cuffed to the bed. She moved her legs between the sheets. Her pants were gone, but her legs weren't bare. Tight, open-toe stockings covered the lower half of her legs. They felt like compression stockings, or TED hose. The ones patients wore after surgery to prevent blood clots.

She lay back against the bed and felt a small warm tube beneath her left thigh. She looked over the edge of the bed and saw a bag hanging from the rail. *A catheter?*

As she lay still, last night started to come back to her. Her brother had pulled up in front of Harry's in his new silver Mercedes. He'd asked her to get in. She probably wouldn't have if it weren't for the secret she was trusting him to keep. The thing she hadn't been brave enough to tell anyone. The secret he'd been threatening to expose. Reluctantly, she got out of the rain and into his car.

He said he wanted to talk to her. *More like interrogate her.* He wanted to know what she was doing at a bar. When she was going to tell mom and dad.

None of it was his business. When she asked him why he'd sent her those emails threatening to blow her secret, he denied it. He even pretended not to know what she was talking about.

She reached for her phone to show him and realized it was gone. She must've dropped it before getting into his car. She told him to stop. Surprisingly, he had. She got out of the car and heard Tyler's new car peel away. Lani turned and started back for Harry's as fast as she could in her four-inch heels. She was half a block from the main road when her brother's car pulled around the corner and parked beside the curb. Apparently, he'd come back to fight some more. But she wasn't in the mood for his petty whining.

He was their parents' golden boy. Their straight-A, perfect child. And he never wanted to let her forget it. Like the way he was flaunting his new Mercedes that she was sure her parents had helped him buy.

She kept walking. Even when she heard his car door slam. She walked faster, ignoring the ache in her feet. Malorie had been right—her heels were too high for walking. He grabbed her arm before she reached the street corner. She started to turn around, ready to shove him away. The blow to the back of her head was the last thing she remembered.

As she looked around, she couldn't imagine he'd do *this*. They'd never liked each other. Always had their differences. As adults, they'd grown to despise each other. But Tyler wasn't a psychopath. If he hadn't sent those emails, then who had?

No matter who had done this to her, she needed to get out. Get free before they came back for her. Who knew what they had planned by keeping her like this? She twisted her wrists and pulled with all her might, trying to get free of the handcuffs. But they were too tight. She thrashed in the bed, yanking her ankles and wrists away from the bed rails.

Exhausted, she finally accepted that there was no way of freeing herself. At least not right now. Her stomach growled as she rested her head against the pillow. As she lay still, she felt the floor steadily rock beneath her bed. It wasn't rough. It was rhythmic.

She wondered if she'd been given something to alter her mind this way. Or was she actually on some kind of boat? From the size of the room, it seemed it would have to be a houseboat. Whatever it was, she needed to find a way to get out.

She could hear the faint sound of traffic nearby. *Where am I?* If only she could scream. She needed to get the duct tape off her mouth. She looked at the window on the wall above her head, covered by dark curtains. It was so close and yet unreachable.

CHAPTER FIVE

Wade lay on his side on the floor, securing the last few screws into the crib. His wife, Elle, had been hanging tiny onesies in the closet for almost as long as he'd been working on the crib. Wade couldn't believe how many clothes she'd been given at her baby shower the day before. His child already had more shirts than Wade, and he wasn't even born yet. This was his last day off before their son's arrival, and he and Elle had spent the day finishing preparations for their newborn.

Wade's phone rang on the opposite side of the room.

"Would you mind handing me that? It might be work."

Elle lifted his phone off the window seat and checked the screen. "It's Malorie," she said, handing it to him.

"Thanks."

He put the call on speaker so he could finish fastening screws while he spoke.

"Hey, Mal."

"Hi, Uncle Wade. Do you have a minute to talk?" Her tone was more serious than usual.

"Sure. What is it?"

"It's my roommate, Lani. She's missing. We went out

last night, and she left the bar with a guy I don't know. They had apparently just started seeing each other. I found her phone on the sidewalk outside the bar right after a silver Mercedes pulled away. And she never came home. She missed an important event today for her mom, and we have a huge midterm tomorrow. There's no way she wouldn't have come back by now if she could help it."

Wade finished tightening the last screw and sat up next to the crib. He took the call off speaker and lifted his phone to his ear.

"Didn't she do this once before? Last May?"

"Well, yeah. But that was different. She's totally changed since then. And she hasn't done anything like that since. I know, it makes it seem like there's less cause for worry, but I know her. She wouldn't do that again. You know how you always say *trust your gut*? My gut tells me she's in trouble."

"How long has she been missing? Since last night?"

"Yeah. About eight o'clock."

"Did you see her get into the silver Mercedes?"

"Um. No. But I'd just gotten off the phone with her before I stepped outside the bar. And when I got to the sidewalk, the Mercedes was pulling away and her phone was on the ground."

"Okay. You didn't happen to get the license plate, did you?"

"No. I didn't think of it at the time."

"That's okay. And you have no idea who she got in the car with?"

"No. She said it was a guy she'd just started seeing. That's all I know."

"Well, if you think something has happened to her, you should go to the West Precinct downtown and file a missing persons report."

"I do."

"Do you want me to go with you?"

"No, that's okay. Thank you."

"Let me know how it goes. Feel free to call me back if you need anything."

"I will. Oh, and how is Elle? When do I get to meet my little cousin?"

Wade could tell she was trying to sound more cheerful than she felt. He looked over at his nine-month-pregnant wife who was filling a drawer with diapers. "She's good. And Friday will be the big day, unless he decides to come sooner."

"I can't wait to meet him. Tell Elle I said hi. I'll keep you updated about Lani."

"Didn't another medical student go missing a few months ago from Elliot Bay University?" Elle asked once Wade was off the phone.

"Yes. And she still hasn't been found."

Wade stood and walked across the room. He wrapped his arms around Elle from behind and placed his palms against her belly. She stopped what she was doing and put her hands on top of his. He leaned over and kissed the side of her head. His life had changed so much since he'd met her a few years ago.

"I feel too tired to cook," Elle said. "How about we go out tonight instead? It might be our last chance for a while."

"Sounds great. Where do you want to go?"

"There's a new Italian place on Capitol Hill. Kayla said it's great."

Wade's phone rang again, and they both knew it could mean he'd be working the rest of the night. He pulled it out of his back pocket and was relieved to see it was Malorie.

"Hey."

"Sorry, Uncle Wade. But my car won't start. I'm not sure why. I can take an Uber to the precinct, but do you think you'd have time in the next few days to take a look at my car?"

Elle could hear Malorie on the other end of the call. She turned to face her husband. "You should go help her," she whispered.

"What about dinner?" he mouthed.

"Go help your niece."

Wade ran his hand up the back of his short black hair. "Mal, I'll be right there. We can go to the precinct together, and then I'll see if I can figure out what's wrong with your car."

He looked down at Elle after hanging up. "Are you sure you'll be okay? Do you want to come?"

She shook her head, looking at his phone. "I'll be fine. That Italian place delivers. And I'm ready to put my feet up anyway. Maybe I'll see if Kayla can come over for a bit. She's been wanting to get together before our little guy comes."

"Your sister will be happy to learn I'm not here."

"Don't say that. She likes you." Elle cracked a smile.

Wade laughed. "You couldn't even say that with a straight face."

"Well, she doesn't *dislike* you. She just needs time. She'll come around."

Wade felt the side of her belly and leaned down to kiss her. "I love you. I'm sorry I haven't been home much lately."

"You're a busy man with an important job to do. I like that about you. Always have. And, right now, your niece needs you more than I do. Unless I go into labor. In that case, you better get your ass home."

CHAPTER SIX

Malorie draped her coat over the back of the living room couch and moved toward Lani's bedroom. Her uncle had picked her up three hours earlier and taken her to the downtown precinct to file Lani's missing persons report. As promised, he'd also fixed her car when they got back. At least temporarily. After looking under her hood and jiggling some wires, he said she'd had a connection issue with the starter. And, if it happened again, she might need a new fuse. Whatever that meant. He sent her a link to order one from Amazon.

She was hoping to get a few more years out of her ten-year-old Mazda. Preferably until she was done with her residency. But, compared to Lani's disappearance, her car trouble seemed trivial.

The young officer who'd processed the report seemed to take Malorie seriously—except for a brief moment after she'd mentioned that Lani's parents had filed a missing persons report on their daughter five months earlier, which turned out to be a false alarm. If the officer had doubts about Lani's disappearance being involuntary, he'd at least kept them to himself. Maybe because her uncle had introduced himself as a sergeant at Seattle Homicide. She was glad he'd gone with her, if only for that reason. The officer who took the report had said a missing persons detective would be in contact with her soon. Probably tomorrow.

Malorie couldn't understand why they wouldn't be in touch with her tonight. Her uncle had tried to explain to her on their way back from the precinct that the lack of urgency was likely due to Lani's previous disappearance. And, although Malorie had felt Lani had changed, there wasn't any evidence to contradict a repeat of that behavior. He reminded her that even Lani's parents weren't concerned yet that she was missing.

Malorie stood in Lani's bedroom doorway and turned on the light. Her bed was unmade, as usual. And still empty. She turned off the light and went into her own room across the hall. Unlike Lani, her bed was made. She smiled, thinking of how opposite she and Lani were. And yet, they were best friends. Most of the time, they brought out the best in each other.

Malorie changed into her oldest, most comfortable sweats and a t-shirt displaying a gray wolf, the university mascot, before she crawled into bed. She pulled her hair tie out of her hair, letting it fall to her shoulders.

She'd gotten up at 5 a.m. to study for tomorrow's midterm. Although exhausted, she couldn't sleep. She hoped her fears were wrong and Lani would saunter into their apartment tomorrow morning as if nothing had happened, just like she'd done last May. But her instincts told her that wasn't going to happen.

Where are you, Lani?

CHAPTER SEVEN

The Seattle skyline glowed orange from the sun rising beyond the city as Detective Blake Stephenson stood over the limbless torso and head that had washed ashore on Alki Beach early Monday morning. The human remains had been discovered by a jogger less than an hour before.

CSI investigators were bent over around the body, documenting the scene and collecting any potential evidence. They had to be careful with a body in this degree of decomposition. Even a gentle touch could cause the victim's skin to slough off. They'd have to wait for Pete, the Medical Examiner, to tell them for sure, but Stephenson guessed their victim had been dead for a couple months.

Having only worked Homicide for two years, this body was the furthest along in decomposition he'd ever seen. And it wasn't pretty. The victim's skin was a greenish-gray, the normal color for a body in the process of decay. There was significant bloating present. The victim's eyes and tongue, which looked to have been nibbled by sea life, protruded out of the face. There was an open wound on the victim's lower abdomen, which also looked to have been eaten away by sea creatures.

From the size and shape, the body looked female. She wore what was left of what appeared to be a hospital gown. Although some of her hair had fallen away from her scalp, shoulder-length strands of black hair were still connected to more than half her head.

"It looks like the victim has a tattoo behind her left ear," one of the CSI investigators said.

Stephenson bent down to get a closer look. It wasn't obvious due to the color the victim's skin had turned, but when he looked carefully, he could see the outline of three stars in a vertical line behind her ear.

Stephenson's partner, Detective Kyle Adams, crouched next to him. "That should help us get a quicker ID," he said. "I'll call Missing Persons and see if they've had any females go missing in the last few months with that tattoo."

Twenty minutes later, the ME was on the scene. Pete's gray curly hair was still damp from the shower.

"Do you think her limbs were cut off before she was dumped in the water?" Stephenson asked as the ME examined the corpse.

He shook his head. "No. It's hard to say for sure, because the limb attachment areas look to have been chewed on by sea life quite a bit. But I would expect the separation of limbs as a normal part of the decomposition process."

"How long do you think she's been dead?"

"Well, as a general rule, bodies decay twice as slow in water than they would in an above-ground environment. As long as the water isn't warm. In waters of these temperatures, where it's been about fifty degrees, I would expect her body to float after a month, maybe a little longer. Given that she either died in the water or was dumped into the Sound shortly after she died. I'll have a better idea after I finish the autopsy, but right now, I'd guess this person's been deceased for at least a month, and possibly closer to two."

"I spoke with Detective Tess Richards from Missing Persons just now," Adams said to the ME.

Hearing his girlfriend's name, Stephenson turned his attention to Adams.

"They had a young woman go missing three months ago with the same star-pattern tattoo behind her ear. She's sending her dental records over to your office." Adams turned to his partner. "The missing woman was a medical student at EBU. Tess said that another female EBU med student went missing over the weekend. They were both Asian. If the dental records are a match to this body, I told her we'll take over her recent missing persons case."

Adams looked down at the discolored, limbless victim lying on the rock-pebbled shore. "And it might mean we'll be looking for a serial killer."

CHAPTER EIGHT

Malorie stared at the door to the lecture hall as she sat in her nine a.m. cardiology class. She'd missed her eight o'clock class to meet with the missing persons detective who'd come to their apartment to get more information about Lani and her disappearance.

She'd introduced herself as Detective Tess Richards. Although the detective looked young, she seemed competent. Malorie had recounted every detail she could about Saturday night to her. The detective had taken Lani's phone and laptop to see if they could find out who she'd left the bar with. Malorie had emailed her photos of Lani that she could send out to other law enforcement and the community. She decided she would make her own *Missing* posters to put up around campus in case anyone else saw who she left the bar with or had any other information.

The detective hadn't seemed very hopeful when she left Malorie's apartment. After answering her questions, Malorie realized how little information she had. The detective said she'd check any surveillance footage Harry's had from Saturday night, but, if Lani's date didn't go inside the bar, she probably wouldn't find anything. Malorie hadn't seen

Lani actually get into the Mercedes even though she was sure she did. And she hadn't thought to get the license plate. All she knew for sure was that it was silver and a two-door. But that didn't exactly narrow it down.

It seemed that if Lani had been taken against her will, the odds of them finding her, or who took her, were not good. The door to the lecture hall swung open and Malorie sat forward in her seat, half-expecting Lani to stroll into class, tired and hungover from a weekend of partying. But it wasn't Lani.

It was Luke Paulson. The hottest guy in their med school cohort, if not in the entire university itself. Every head in the room turned, including the professor's, as Luke walked through the lecture hall to find a seat, fifteen minutes after the class had started.

Malorie watched him stride across the room. He stood a few inches over six feet and had the build of an athlete. His sandy brown hair almost matched the color of his eyes. Around campus, his looks had earned him the nickname *McSteamy* from the popular Seattle-based TV series, *Grey's Anatomy*.

The professor paused briefly from the interruption but continued without remarking on Luke's tardiness. Luke plopped into the empty seat next to Malorie that she'd saved for Lani. Just in case. Luke smiled at Malorie after he'd taken his seat, flashing his movie star-white teeth. Malorie returned his smile and pretended to go back to listening to the lecture.

Malorie saw Lani's ex-boyfriend, Dante, sitting in the front row of the lecture hall. She wondered if he might somehow be connected to her disappearance. Would he have taken her? He didn't drive a Mercedes. And he'd been the one to break up with Lani. He'd also seemed to have moved on since then. Malorie had seen him around campus with his arm around a short brunette.

"You ready for our midterm?" Luke asked, following Malorie out of the lecture hall.

She'd almost forgotten. "I think so."

They walked down the concrete steps to the courtyard outside the Health Sciences building. The university's foliage had turned different shades of fall colors. The maple trees that lined the courtyard were starting to lose their leaves that had become stunning shades of gold, copper, and orange. A beautiful sight if you weren't consumed by the disappearance of your best friend.

"A few of us are going to hit the library, if you want to join us for some last-minute cramming."

She met his gaze, noticing he was even more attractive up close than he was at a distance. Despite having almost every class together for the last two and a half years, Malorie had never spoken to him before.

"Actually, I do better studying alone. But thanks for the offer."

"All right. You know where to find us if you change your mind." He flashed her one last smile before he turned for the library.

Malorie walked straight through the courtyard, heading for her and Lani's apartment. If Lani had been with her, she would have berated Malorie for not accepting Luke's invite, even if it was only to a group study. Lani had always been more flirtatious and forward with men. She often chided Malorie for not dating enough and for being too focused on school. Ironically, if it weren't for Lani's disappearance, Malorie *would've* joined Luke in the library.

She'd been awake most of last night worrying about her roommate. There was only one hour before the midterm. She needed some caffeine and to look over her notes without any distractions.

Malorie cut through the faculty parking lot but stopped short when she spotted a silver two-door Mercedes. The car's taillights flashed. She turned to see Dr. Delaney, her anesthesiology professor walking toward the car.

"It's Malorie, right?"

She turned back to the Mercedes, unable to take her eyes away. It wasn't the sight of the silver Mercedes that kept her attention, it was the dark red dots smeared across the left side of the rear bumper. They looked like dried blood.

"Are you okay?" he asked when she didn't respond.

She needed to call the missing persons detective. "Yes." Malorie forced herself to look away from the bumper and meet her professor's gaze.

He looked at her curiously before rounding the driver's side of the Mercedes, giving no attention to the small streaks on the back of his car. "I'll see you in an hour for the midterm."

Malorie stood in the middle of the parking lot and watched him pull away. She didn't have time to get her phone out of her bag to take a picture, so she memorized his license plate until she could open the notepad in her phone. Then, she called the detective she'd met earlier that morning.

She answered on the first ring. "Detective Richards."

"Hi, it's Malorie." She told her what she'd seen on the back of her professor's car that was exactly like the one Lani had gotten in on Saturday night.

"Well, to test it, we'd have to get a search warrant, unless he gives us his consent. And I'm not sure we have enough grounds for that. For one thing, we don't know that it's blood."

"I'm sure it was blood."

"Can you text me a picture?"

"No, he drove away. But he'll be back within an hour. He has a class."

"We also don't know that it was the car Lani got into, other than being the same make and model."

"And color," Malorie added.

"Right. But you didn't actually see her get into the Mercedes. Like you, I believe that she probably did, but I don't think that's enough to justify a warrant."

"Could you ask for his consent and see what he says?"

The detective breathed into the phone. "I could, but if it *is* Lani's blood, he'd be an idiot to say yes. I'm at Harry's getting their surveillance footage from Saturday night. They don't have any outside cameras, so we're not going to see her get into the car. But we might see if she met anyone inside the bar. You said you got the license plate for that Mercedes?"

"Yes." She read her the plate numbers she'd typed into her phone.

"Let me see what we've got for surveillance footage, and I'll check out that license plate. If that *is* evidence on his car, maybe I can find a little more cause for a search warrant before we go pointing it out to him, okay? I'd also like to see it before I try for a warrant."

"Okay. I have a midterm in an hour, but I can meet you in the faculty parking lot by the Health Sciences building before then. I'm sure it's where he'll park when he comes back."

"All right. I'll call you when I get there."

Malorie was filled with questions as she walked through the campus. *Had Dr. Delaney been Lani's date on Saturday night? Was that why she'd been so secretive about it? Since when did she go out with married men twice her age? Was he the reason she was given a second chance last semester? No, Lani wouldn't do that.* Unless she didn't know her friend as well as she thought she did.

And the blood on his car. Could it mean Lani was dead? That Dr. Delaney had killed her? That seemed crazy. But it didn't mean it wasn't true. She could only hope Detective Richards would find a reason to be able to test the Mercedes for Lani's blood.

Malorie turned on her coffee pot when she got back to her apartment. She had only forty minutes before her midterm, and she couldn't afford to fail it. Not if she wanted to be a doctor. She sat on her couch and tried to go over her study notes. She looked over the cheat sheet she'd made from the midterm study topics but found herself staring at the page, unable to concentrate.

She picked up her phone, deciding to check the local news for anything that could be related to Lani. She covered her mouth with her hand when she read the headline on the local news.

UNIDENTIFIED HEAD AND TORSO FOUND ON SEATTLE SHORELINE.

There was a smaller headline from another article underneath it.

Are the human remains washed ashore on Alki Beach those of missing EBU student?

Malorie choked back the vomit that rose to the back of her throat and clicked on the article. Her screen changed before the article loaded. *Incoming Call - Uncle Wade.* She took

VIABLE HOSTAGE

a deep breath before she answered.

CHAPTER NINE

"Is it Lani?"

"I was hoping you hadn't read the news yet," Wade said. "No, it isn't Lani. That's why I called. I didn't want you to worry. The person we found on Alki Beach has been dead for a couple months. So, it's definitely not Lani."

"Why did an article speculate that it was a missing EBU student?"

"We haven't ID'd the body yet, so the media shouldn't be speculating anything. But there was another Elliot Bay University student who went missing about three months ago. She was also a med student. Fourth year. The timeline fits, but we are waiting for the medical examiner to confirm dental records."

Of course, how did she not think about that before? *Tina Lang*. It had been all over the news. She'd gone missing at the end of the summer. Being a fourth-year med student, Malorie hadn't known her, but she'd recognized her photo from seeing her around campus. She'd been so consumed by Lani's disappearance that somehow she hadn't thought about the connection.

"Do you think her disappearance is related to Lani's?

Maybe they were taken by the same person."

"We don't know yet. There wasn't much to go on in Tina Lang's missing persons report. But if the body does turn out to be Tina Lang, then I'm going to suggest Lani's case get turned over to Homicide since they were both EBU med students and went missing three months apart."

Malorie struggled to take in what her uncle was telling her. "So, you think Lani's dead?"

"Not necessarily, no. And, right now, we don't even know if the body is Tina's. But, if it is, then it's possible the person who killed her is also involved in Lani's disappearance, so that will need to be investigated. I have to go, but I'll update you when I can, okay?"

"Okay." Malorie stared at her phone screen after the call ended. She'd been so rattled by the news of Tina Lang that she'd forgotten to tell him about the blood on Dr. Delaney's Mercedes. Although she figured that was probably all right. Lani wasn't his case, and she'd already told Detective Richards.

She had almost finished reading through the second article about the limbless torso and head that a jogger had found on the shores of Alki Beach earlier that morning when another call came through her phone. *Detective Richards.*

"I'm here," the detective said after Malorie answered. "I'm parked near the Health Sciences building. I think I've found the faculty parking lot. That's where you saw the Mercedes, right?"

She'd forgotten about asking her to come to the university to look at Dr. Delaney's car. It felt like so long ago that she'd called her.

"Great. I'll be right there. I'm just leaving my

apartment." She stuffed her notes back into her bag.

Malorie was out of breath when she got to the parking lot less than ten minutes later. Just as she'd said, Detective Richards was waiting for her. Her blonde hair shone against the late October sun. She was standing a few feet away from Dr. Delaney's Mercedes. It was parked back in the same spot.

"You can tell it's blood, right?" Malorie asked when she got closer to her.

She pointed to the Mercedes. "This is the car?"

She followed her finger to the Mercedes. "Yeah, it's—" Malorie saw why she was asking. She stepped closer to the car's rear bumper. She bent down, bringing her face within inches of the bumper's clean, shiny exterior.

She turned to the detective. "He must've washed it. He saw me looking at his car. He must've taken it through a car wash." She stood and put both hands on her head. "I can't believe it. This proves it was blood though. That he's hiding something. That he took Lani, and now he's trying to cover it up."

Detective Richards stared at the bumper without a response. Malorie moved toward her.

"Right?"

"I'm afraid it doesn't prove anything. Other than he washed his car."

"Please tell me you're kidding. You can still test it. There could still be trace amounts of her blood on there. And we haven't even looked inside the car, or the trunk. Or under the car."

"I'm not saying I don't believe you. I do. But this doesn't give me enough cause for a warrant to process the car. I'm going to need something more. But I'll keep looking. I'm still gathering information."

"Is this because his wife is the president of the university?"

"No, but I did learn that before I came over. What was his relationship to Lani? He's one of her professors? Was there anything more that you know of?"

"They didn't have a relationship that I knew of. Other than him being one of our professors."

"I'll see if I can ask him some questions while I'm here. What time is the class?"

"It's from eleven to twelve."

Malorie checked the time on her phone. *11:15*. She swore and tossed her phone into her bag.

"I'm late for my midterm. Sorry, but I have to run. His office is on the second level of that building." She pointed to the nineteenth-century, stone-covered building adjacent to the parking lot before she jogged across the courtyard.

Please don't be locked. Please don't be locked. Malorie ran down one of the main hallways in the Health Sciences building. A sign covered the window on the door to Dr. Delaney's class: *EXAM IN PROGRESS*. She tried the door handle, but, as she'd feared, it didn't move. Most of her medical school professors had a policy of locking the doors to their lecture halls during an exam to minimize interruptions.

She leaned against the wall in the empty hallway. She'd never been late for an exam. Ever. She'd have to talk to Dr. Delaney. Hopefully, he'd be understanding. Her medical degree might depend on it.

And maybe ask him about the blood on his car. She sank to the floor and waited for the last student to leave the lecture hall. She pulled herself to her feet and held the door open as she watched Dr. Delaney gather all the tests and file them into his briefcase.

He didn't notice her standing there. She tried to gather her thoughts about asking him to give her another chance to take the exam. She also debated about whether to accuse him of kidnapping Lani. Or worse.

The more she thought about it, it seemed ridiculous to accuse a distinguished doctor and faculty member of something like that. But, ridiculous as it was, Lani was still missing and there was no mistaking what she had seen on the back of his car. Malorie cleared her throat and approached the professor.

CHAPTER TEN

Stephenson stood from his desk across from his partner in the cubicle they shared at the Homicide Unit. He stretched his arms behind his back. Since they'd gotten back from the crime scene at Alki Beach, he and Adams had been going over the missing persons reports from both their assumed victim, Tina Lang, and her cohort who'd gone missing over the weekend, Lani Wu.

Aside from their appearance and both being medical students, the two women didn't seem to have much in common. Tina Lang was a Chinese citizen who'd been living in America for the last seven and a half years on an international student visa. She was a straight-A student, had an almost nonexistent social life, and no current boyfriend. All her family was still in China.

Like Lani, Tina had been living in an on-campus apartment when she'd gone missing in August. Because the fall semester hadn't yet started, there were substantially fewer people living on campus at the time. Tina had told her roommate she was going out around seven p.m. on Thursday, August fifteenth and hadn't been seen or heard from since. Her car had remained in its on-campus parking spot, and there was no trace of Tina on any of the campus's security footage from that night.

American-born Lani Wu, however, had a reputation of being a partier. This was the second time a missing persons report had been filed on her in the last six months, after the first report the previous spring turned out to be a false alarm when she'd disappeared on a drug and alcohol binge. According to her roommate who'd filed the latest report, Lani had nearly flunked out of med school after it happened but had been on the straight and narrow ever since.

Coincidentally, Stephenson had also learned that Lani's roommate, Malorie, was his Sergeant Wade McKinnon's niece.

"Remember the skeletal hand that crabber found off Bainbridge Island last July?" Adams smiled. "In the pincher of a crab claw when he pulled up his pot?"

Stephenson wasn't sure what there was to smile about. "Yeah, I remember." The hand couldn't have been Tina Lang's; she didn't go missing until six weeks after the hand was found. But, if we *were* looking for a serial killer who was dumping bodies in the Sound, it could be related.

"I wonder if the Bainbridge detectives have gotten DNA back yet," Adams said.

"You want me to call?"

"That's all right, I'll do it."

"Okay. I'm going to walk over to the ME's office and see if I can attend the rest of the autopsy."

They were still waiting on Pete to confirm Tina's identity with her dental records before they could notify her family.

"You want to join me after you make that call?" Stephenson asked.

"No, thanks. I'll let you enlighten me when you come

back."

Stephenson wasn't surprised, but it was something that bothered him about his partner. He never attended victim autopsies. It wasn't a requirement of detectives, but there was a lot more to be learned firsthand than just reading the ME's autopsy report. Adams wasn't a bad detective, and he'd worked Homicide about fifteen years longer than Stephenson. But some of his practices struck Stephenson as complacent. This being one of them.

"Suit yourself," Stephenson said, pulling on his suit jacket. His desk phone rang as he turned to leave.

"Detective Stephenson."

"Blake, it's Pete. I'm still completing the autopsy, but there are a couple things I thought you should know. First, I've confirmed with dental X-rays the identity of the body. The X-rays were a match to Tina Lang."

"Okay. What's the second thing?"

"It appears the wound on her abdomen had been initially made as a surgical incision. It's impossible to tell from the surface since fish have picked apart the superficial layer of the wound. But, after I started the autopsy, I discovered that her uterus had been sliced open. A clean, straight cut made by a scalpel or something similar. I would conjecture to say that whoever made the incision had medical training. It's a classical incision, which isn't the most common. It's used mainly for an emergent delivery or the delivery of an extremely preterm infant.

"Because the uterus is one of the last internal organs to succumb to decay, I was able to obtain some placental fragments. From the size of her uterus, I would estimate that she was about five months pregnant. Give or take a month."

Stephenson hadn't seen anything in Tina's missing persons report that said she was pregnant.

"There is absolutely no healing of the uterine wall," Pete went on. "No scar tissue whatsoever. There's also no evidence there was any attempt to suture or close her wound. Unless I find something else, my best guess at her cause of death would be that she bled out through her incision."

"So, someone cut her baby out and left her to bleed to death?"

Adams looked up from his search for the Bainbridge detective's phone number.

"Yes. Probably someone with medical training. She might've been anesthetized or sedated for whoever did it to be able to make a clean incision of her uterus."

"And would her infant have been viable?"

"Possibly. It depends on exactly how far along she was. But I doubt it would've survived without being in a neonatal intensive care unit."

"Okay."

"That's all I have for now. I'll let you know when I've finished the autopsy."

"Thanks, Pete."

Adams was staring at him when he hung up with the Medical Examiner.

"She was pregnant? And someone cut her open, stole her baby, and left her to bleed to death?"

"Yes. Except Pete thinks she was only about five months pregnant, give or take a month. So, her baby wouldn't have survived without being in a neonatal intensive care unit. Even then, she might not have been far enough along for it to be viable. And, he confirmed that she is Tina Lang."

"There isn't anything in her report about being pregnant," Adams said.

Or Lani's, Stephenson thought. They'd have to ask Lani's family and McKinnon's niece if there was any indication that Lani might be pregnant too. But first, they needed to notify Tina's parents. Looks like he wouldn't be attending her autopsy after all.

CHAPTER ELEVEN

Lani awoke to darkness. It only took her a moment to remember where she was. She screamed into the large pieces of duct tape that covered her mouth. The only noise that escaped was too muffled to attract any attention. The tape covered her face from the base of her nose to her chin and had been wrapped tightly around the back of her head more than once. She sat forward on her bed and stretched her back.

She tried to adjust her eyes to the darkness around her. *How long have I been asleep?* It was all so crazy she almost thought she was dreaming.

She prayed someone was looking for her. Her parents would probably think she was just being her normal irresponsible self, but Malorie would know different. She wondered if the police would even take Malorie seriously if she filed a missing persons report. It would be the second one filed on her in the last six months. And she had no one to blame for that but herself.

If she wanted to live, she needed to escape. She knew enough to be certain her captor was one sick freak. Her thoughts were interrupted when light flooded the room.

She squinted and turned toward the door. Her captor was dressed in surgical scrubs and a white lab coat. His hair was covered by a blue surgical hat, and his face by a surgical mask and tinted protective glasses. Her eyes moved to his hands, covered by blue disposable gloves. In his right hand, he held a small handgun.

She watched him move casually toward her bed. He didn't speak as he strode toward her.

He aimed his gun at her head while he pulled a small set of keys out of his scrub pocket. He unlocked her ankles first. He waited a moment before unlocking her hands, making sure she wasn't going to fight. He removed her handcuffs from the bed rails but kept the cuffs around her wrists. Instead of freeing her hands, he linked the two cuffs together.

He pulled back her blanket, exposing her white, knee-high stockings. They were just as she'd thought. Hospital-grade TED hose.

He grabbed her by the upper arm, and she allowed him to pull her to her feet. She looked down at her belly when she stood. Even in the hospital gown, there was no hiding her growing bump. Her captor leaned over. He grabbed her catheter bag and held it out for her to hold.

He lowered the gun so the barrel pointed at her chest as she grabbed hold of the bag with her cuffed hands. He wrapped his free hand around her IV pole. He swung his gun toward the exercise machine before returning its aim to her chest. He rolled her IV pole toward the treadmill.

Lani moved at the same speed as her IV pole. The man walked beside her the few steps it took to cross the small room. Lani wondered if she should try to get his gun away from him. But, with her hands cuffed together, she'd likely end up getting shot. She had no reason to doubt he would kill her. She stepped onto the belt of the treadmill, deciding to wait for a better moment to try and get the upper hand.

He turned on the treadmill, slowly at first, and then increased it to a brisk walk. Lani struggled to keep up the pace with her hands cuffed in front of her.

Why are you so concerned with me getting blood clots if you're just going to kill me? she wondered. *Why are you keeping me alive?*

With the duct tape over her mouth, she had no way of asking him. She turned to look at him. She couldn't be sure if he was her brother. His face was completely covered by his medical gear.

After fifteen minutes, he turned the treadmill off.

She allowed him to help her off the machine and imprison her to the bed once again. Without a word, he left the room. But he left the door open. A minute later, he returned. Instead of a gun, he held something small and white in his hand.

He approached her bed and lifted her hospital gown above her navel. He squirted a cold gel onto her lower abdomen and pressed what she recognized to be a Doppler to her stomach. After a minute, she heard the rhythmic swoosh of her baby's heartbeat come through the monitor in his hand.

Satisfied, he pulled the Doppler away from her belly. He silently wiped the gel away with a tissue before pulling her blanket up to her waist.

He started to leave the room but turned back. He used a remote to turn on the small flat screen on the wall at the end of her bed. He scrolled through the channels on the TV guide. He looked down at her before selecting a home and garden channel.

The show went to a commercial, and her captor stood and watched before he let out a lighthearted chuckle. Lani racked her brain to think if she recognized his laugh, but she caught nothing she recognized. She couldn't even be sure it wasn't Tyler.

Lani watched him with disgust as he set the remote in the treadmill's cup holder without a word. He turned off the lights when he left the room. This time, he closed the door behind him.

Lani tried to scream as loudly as she could. She tried screaming her brother's name, in case it was him. She thrashed back and forth in the bed, desperately trying to free herself from this prison. Her lungs burned from her effort, even though the only sound she produced was overpowered by the TV.

That sick bastard. He was only keeping her alive to keep her baby alive. Her little girl. The thought made her nauseous. What was he planning to do with her baby? Sell her on the black market? She hadn't been sure of the dates, but her doctor estimated she was only twenty-two weeks along. Was he going to keep her here for the rest of her pregnancy? And then kill her?

She'd been so scared when she found out at the start of last summer. It was the reason she hadn't told anyone. Especially her family.

She and Dante had already been broken up for over a month when she'd taken the pregnancy test. He'd been so horrible to her when he'd ended their relationship. Among other things, he'd accused her of sleeping with a professor to save herself from flunking out of med school. It wasn't true, but he wouldn't tell her who had planted that idea in his head.

VIABLE HOSTAGE

She supposed it was her fault for getting herself such a wild reputation that he believed it. She still hadn't told him she was pregnant, knowing he'd probably deny the child was his anyway.

At first, she worried she might not finish med school. That she'd be an even bigger disappointment to her parents than she already was. But she'd come to realize that none of that mattered. She didn't care. She was a mother. And that was going to come first. Before anything else.

It was getting harder to hide, and she was planning to tell Malorie and her family after her mother's award ceremony that weekend. Now, she feared she might never have the chance.

She looked around the room. Her head stopped when she noticed something beneath the treadmill catching the light from the TV. She sat forward, focusing on the flat object. It took her a moment to recognize what it was. A scalpel. The early morning sun that shone through the window above her head allowed her to see its shiny blade.

There was no way she was going to let him take her baby. Not even over her dead body. She needed to get out.

She hadn't tried to fight him that morning because she was afraid she might die if she did. She knew now it was a chance she'd have to take. What other choice did she have?

CHAPTER TWELVE

The man pulled off his surgical mask after locking the door to Lani's room. He took off his disposable gloves and checked the time on his watch. He had less than two hours before he had to be at the university, and his work was far from done.

He removed his surgical glasses as he walked down the houseboat's narrow hallway. He didn't *have* to conceal his identity. But he felt it might give her some false sense of hope, which would help keep her safely subdued. She could never get free, but he supposed it also gave him some insurance in the near-impossible event she managed to escape.

He stepped into the room, down the hall from Lani's, where he conducted his research. Tina's baby's vitals were stable, which was a huge relief after almost losing her over the weekend. He stepped closer to the clear, sterile bag lying atop the padded, temperature-controlled mobile support platform that contained the thirty-week-old fetus. She was sleeping soundly.

The bag was filled with a synthetic amniotic fluid. A filtered pump was connected to the bag on either side which constantly recirculated the transparent electrolyte solution. Her IVs were running smoothly through her umbilical catheters that he'd placed in her umbilical vein and artery through a porthole in the bag shortly after she was born.

Her umbilical vessels were also connected to a pumpless aterio-venous circuit that allowed the blood flow to be driven by the fetal heart. The circuit incorporated a simple, low-resistance oxygenator and simulated the circulation between a fetus and placenta.

He took note of her heart rate and blood pressure on the monitor, obtained through her umbilical arterial catheter. When her heart rate increased and blood pressure dropped over the weekend, he'd quickly recognized the early symptoms of sepsis. As careful as he'd been to maintain a sterile technique when accessing the ports in her bag, some bacteria had gotten through. Due to her immature immune system, he knew she was at high risk of developing an infection. He'd wasted no time in administering the antibiotics he'd already kept on hand for that kind of situation.

He could've lost her, but she pulled through. Her coinciding fragility and resilience amazed him. Her vitals had gotten worse before they improved. He was happy to see that her blood pressure was holding steady despite being off the vasopressors for the last twelve hours.

He walked to the small fridge in the corner of the room and pulled out a fresh bag of IV fluids. He carefully donned sterile gloves before spiking the bag and priming new IV tubing. He changed into fresh sterile gloves before he connected the new tubing to her umbilical arterial line.

To think, she was only his second subject, and she was doing incredibly well. Even better than he'd hoped. The first infant he'd used for his research had died only days after he'd taken him from his mother's uterus.

When he met the mother, Gretchen, he saw an opportunity to take someone who wouldn't be missed and put her existence toward good use. He'd done her a service, really. Given some meaning to her life.

The first time, he'd underestimated the difficulty of transferring the fetus to the bag with no extra hands to help him. He'd realized too late that he was missing some supplies and ended up contaminating his sterile field during his attempt to stabilize the infant after birth. By the time he'd gotten the twenty-two-week fetus into the sterile bag, the subject was already compromised. He'd stressed the tiny neonate during the less-than-smooth transfer. By the time he took an arterial blood gas sample, the fetus was already acidotic.

He ended up rushing the placement of the umbilical catheters, and, in hindsight, knew he'd failed to maintain a sterile field in the process. The infant had succumbed to septic shock three days later. But his death hadn't been for nothing. He had learned from the experience. And, because of it, Tina's baby was thriving—contrary to his fear that he might have a few more die before he obtained a favorable outcome.

After resetting the IV pump and ensuring the infant had enough fluids to last until he got back from the university, the man stepped back to admire his work. Aside from nearly losing her that weekend, his research trial was, so far, a huge success.

CHAPTER THIRTEEN

Malorie moved the stack of posters she'd made seeking information about Lani's disappearance to make room for her bowl of top ramen on her coffee table. After her last class got out, she'd spent the rest of the afternoon putting the posters up around campus. She could only hope someone saw Lani get in the car with Dr. Delaney on Saturday night.

She opened her laptop to go through a Power Point for her radiology midterm tomorrow. But before she opened the presentation, she decided to look up Dr. Delaney. She searched his name on the university website. An article came up with a photo of him standing next to his wife, the president of the university. She clicked on a link to his faculty bio page.

He smiled confidently in his photo, looking better in the picture than he did in person. His salt-and-pepper hair was short and neat, and the photo hid the extra fifty pounds he carried around. Looking at his face made Malorie feel sick. Her thoughts were going crazy imagining what he'd done to Lani.

Her talk with him after she missed his midterm had gone

well. She held back from accusing him of anything, and he agreed to let her retake the midterm tomorrow afternoon after his class. He'd even acted sympathetic about Lani's disappearance. The son of a bitch.

Malorie opened a new window on her laptop and typed *Dr. Jerad Delaney* into an Internet search engine. She scrolled through the results related to his wife and his academic achievements. She stopped when she saw a news article from nearly eight years ago.

DOCTOR AND UNIVERSITY PROFESSOR FOUND NOT GUILTY OF RAPE ALLEGATIONS.

She clicked the link and leaned closer to the screen.

Anesthesiologist Jerad Delaney was found not guilty by a jury of the rape of his medical student, Rosario Ocampo. Ocampo accused him of drugging her during a private meeting in his university office and then raping her. The prosecution claimed that Ocampo waited a month to report the assault, due to fear that accusing a professor might jeopardize her medical degree.

The lead counsel for Dr. Delaney's defense issued the following statement regarding today's verdict: We are very pleased with today's verdict. We hope it has restored faith in Jerad for any who doubted him against these false accusations. Today, justice has prevailed.

There was a photo of Rosario Ocampo, the student who'd accused him, at the end of the article. She had long, black hair just like Lani's. She looked like she was of southeast Asian descent. Maybe Filipino.

So, Dr. Delaney had a type. And a track record. Malorie closed out of the article. She returned to her search results to see what else she could find on the trial. She was about to click on another article when her phone vibrated on the couch next to her.

She didn't recognize the number, but she answered anyway. It could be about Lani.

"This is Malorie."

"Hi, Malorie. This is Detective Blake Stephenson from the Seattle Homicide Unit. We still haven't found Lani, but my partner and I have taken her case over from Missing Persons. Are you free for me to come by and ask you some questions?"

They must think Lani's disappearance was related to Tina's death. Just as her uncle had warned her. "Yes. I'm at home. I'll be here for the rest of the night. Just call me when you get here. I'll come meet you downstairs."

"Great. I'll be there soon. Thank you."

Malorie filled the time after they got off the phone reading everything she could find about the student who'd accused Dr. Delaney of rape. She'd found several more articles.

Rosario had taken the witness stand during the trial and stated that Dr. Delaney had called her into his private office to discuss her exam results. She admitted that her grades had been slipping that semester. She was afraid of failing his class and not graduating med school. When she got to his office, the blinds were drawn. He offered her a glass of bourbon before their meeting started. Rosario said she declined at first, but he insisted. She hadn't wanted to offend him, so she obliged.

By the time she'd finished the drink, the room was spinning. She was light-headed and felt like she needed to lie down. He helped her to the couch in his office. He turned off the lights and told her she could rest as long as she wanted.

She passed out. When she awoke several hours later, the room was dark and she was alone. She was naked from the waist down. She'd found her pants and underwear strewn on the floor next to the couch. She was still disoriented and dizzy from being drugged, and it took her several minutes to get dressed.

She stumbled back to her one-bedroom on-campus apartment, in shock of what had been done to her. She had no recollection of being raped, but she could feel the residual pain from her professor forcing himself inside her. She knew she should report it, but she was scared.

Her attorneys stated at the trial that she was afraid no one would believe her. She hadn't wanted to jeopardize her future as a doctor. And, when she'd gotten back to her apartment, she was still under the influence of the heavy sedation she'd been given.

It took her a month before she got up the courage to report the attack. At that point, it was too late to complete a rape kit or a toxicology screen to determine what she'd been drugged with.

Dr. Delaney's highly paid attorneys painted Rosario as a conniving, irresponsible student taking desperate measures as a way to stay in med school despite her failing grades. In the end, they won. And Dr. Delaney had been freed of all charges and allowed to continue to prey on his female students. Malorie was livid.

Twenty-five minutes later, Malorie was happy to see that her uncle had come along with Detective Stephenson when she let them into the lobby of her building. In that moment, Malorie was struck by how much her uncle looked like her mom. Malorie had always looked more like her American Samoan father than her African American mother.

"I was free, so I thought I'd come along," her uncle said. "Can we go to your apartment so we can talk in private?"

"Of course."

As they rode the elevator to the fifth floor, Malorie noticed both men looked tired. She realized she probably did too.

"Feel free to have a seat," she told them when they got inside her apartment.

They sat in the two chairs opposite the couch, where Malorie took a seat. Her bowl of ramen noodles lay untouched atop the coffee table. She looked across at Detective Stephenson. Like Detective Richards, he looked young for a detective, probably only a few years older than herself.

"First of all," he said. "I want you to know that Lani's case has been transferred to Homicide because we think it's possible that she was taken by the same person who murdered Tina Lang. But we could be wrong. And we don't have any evidence at this point that Lani is dead."

Malorie took a deep breath. "Okay. Did Detective Richards tell you about the blood I saw on Dr. Delaney's Mercedes? The same car that Lani left the bar in on Saturday night? Are you going to process his car? Or arrest him?"

"She did, yes. And she spoke with Dr. Delaney earlier today. He has an alibi for Saturday night. He was in Spokane. Detective Richards verified that he spoke at a conference in Spokane on Saturday and spent the night in a hotel on Saturday night. He didn't return to Seattle until Sunday afternoon."

That couldn't be right. "He's lying. He has to be."

"We have video footage of him at the Spokane hotel on Saturday and Sunday."

Malorie's head was reeling. That didn't make any sense. She knew he'd taken Lani. She looked at her uncle and then Detective Stephenson.

"So, you're not even going to search Dr. Delaney's car? Maybe he drove back to Seattle Saturday night, took Lani, and then went back to Spokane to have an alibi. I know what I saw. It was blood. And as soon as he realized that I noticed it, he took the car through a car wash. He's guilty. He took Lani. I know it."

"We can't argue with the video footage. He was seen on camera at the hotel within thirty minutes of when Lani was picked up from the bar," her uncle said. "You saw a silver Mercedes. But, without the license plate, you can't be sure whose car it was."

"What did he say about the blood on his car? Did Detective Richards ask him about that?"

"She did," Stephenson said. "Dr. Delaney denied seeing anything that looked like blood on his bumper. He admitted to getting his car washed, but only because it was dirty. We can't arrest him for that."

I know what I saw, Malorie thought. "Did you know he raped one of his students eight years ago?"

"We know about the trial, but he was found not guilty."

"I guess with enough money, you can get away with almost anything."

Neither of the two men refuted her statement.

"We haven't released this information yet to the public, but, during her autopsy, the Medical Examiner found that Tina was pregnant," the young detective said. "It looks like her pregnancy might've been connected to her death. My partner is in the process of obtaining a warrant for Lani's medical records, but it will take a day or so before we have them. We've already spoken with Lani's parents, and they didn't believe Lani was pregnant. But, since you and Lani were so close, I wanted to ask you also. Were you aware if Lani was pregnant?"

"Pregnant? No. No way. We're in medical school." Malorie shook her head. "And I know she would've told me if she were."

"And Lani didn't have a boyfriend?"

"No. She had a steady boyfriend for four years. Dante. He's in our med school cohort. But he broke up with her in May. Their breakup served as a wake up call for her, in addition to almost failing one of her classes last semester. She's changed since then. I haven't seen her drink in months."

Her uncle and Detective Stephenson exchanged a look.

"But not because she's pregnant. Because she's become a different person. She's had casual dates, but no steady boyfriend since Dante. And there's no way she would've hid it from me if she was pregnant."

"Okay," Stephenson said. "Did she and Dante end on good terms?"

Malorie shrugged her shoulders. "As far as I know." Lani had never given her much of an explanation for why he'd broken up with her. Either Dante hadn't given Lani much of a reason, or Lani was embarrassed and didn't want her to know. "Why do you think Tina's pregnancy was related to her death?"

Stephenson folded his hands in his lap. "Tina had an abdominal wound. A classical c-section incision. The Medical Examiner found retained placental fragments in her uterus, but no fetus. It appeared there had been no attempt to close the incision. The ME hasn't given us an official cause of death yet, but it looks like she bled out through the incision."

Malorie stared at the detective, her hand covering her mouth. "Someone cut Tina's baby out and left her to die?"

"It appears that way, yes."

"And you think if Lani is pregnant that the same thing is going to happen to her?"

"We're exploring the possibility."

"Well, she's not pregnant. I'm positive. She wouldn't keep something like that from me."

"Thanks for answering our questions, Mal," her uncle said.

The two men stood from their chairs. Stephenson held out his card to her. "If you think of anything else, feel free to call me."

She took the card and followed them to the door. "I will." She stood in her doorway and watched them walk to the elevator. "Please find her."

They turned.

"We'll do our best," Stephenson said.

She leaned her head against the door frame and looked down at the business card Stephenson had given her after they got in the elevator at the end of the hall. She hoped his "best" would be enough to find her friend. And that Lani would still be alive when he did.

CHAPTER FOURTEEN

Jerad Delaney stood in a bathroom stall in the OR men's locker room at Elliot Bay University Medical Center. He was three hours into his twelve-hour night shift. There were no more surgeries scheduled for the night. He was hoping to get some rest in the Sleep Room while he stayed on call for emergencies.

He'd received the video message on his phone after taking his last patient to PACU, the post-anesthesia care unit, after their spinal fusion surgery. Seeing the sender's number, he'd been afraid to open the video in the halls of the hospital. This was the second time he'd received a message from this number. The first had been three months ago. Right after Tina Lang went missing.

There was a one-sentence caption under the video. *Say anything and the world will know what you've done.* He didn't have to guess what she was referring to. The blood she'd left on his car had been no accident. It was a message. She'd wanted him to know what she'd done.

He should've known better than to switch cars with her last weekend. But the cruise control in his Mercedes wasn't working, and it seemed like a good idea to take her 4-wheel drive over Snoqualmie Pass since there'd been a slight chance of snow. He didn't think she would use his car to kidnap one of his students. Or worse.

Thankfully, he had an alibi.

He'd seen the news that morning about the body parts that had washed ashore on Alki Beach. When he learned that afternoon that they'd identified the remains as Tina Lang, he was stunned. He'd suspected his wife of twenty years to have something to do with her disappearance. But now he knew for sure that she'd killed her.

It was her way of punishing him. Her sociopathic revenge. Taking women that looked like the students he'd preyed on. And killing them. Then blackmailing him.

He heard someone come into the locker room. He made sure the video was muted before he pressed play. The hidden camera captured a woman, his student, lying on the couch in his office at the university. Her arm hung off the side onto the floor. She lay still, semi-conscious, with her eyes barely open. She was still clothed, wearing an above-the-knee dress.

He watched himself come into the camera's viewpoint. He walked to the office door and turned the lock. He turned and knelt over the woman, reached under her dress, and slipped off her underwear, tossing them on the floor beside the couch. He stood up and unbuckled his belt before unzipping his pants. His pants and boxers fell to his ankles. He lifted her dress as he climbed on top of her.

Jerad stopped the video, knowing what was about to happen next. Plus, the video had lost its appeal knowing his wife had sent it to him as insurance to not narc on her killing spree.

VIABLE HOSTAGE

He deleted the video and slid his phone into the pocket of his scrubs. From the same pocket, he pulled out the nearly full vial of fentanyl he'd saved from that night's operation. He swiftly removed a needle and syringe from their packaging and withdrew the vial's contents.

He pulled up the sleeve of the shirt under his scrubs and injected the solution into a vein in his upper arm. After smoothly recapping the needle, he dropped the empty syringe and vial back into his pocket. He used a small, balled-up piece of toilet paper to apply pressure to his needle puncture site.

The urinal flushed next to his stall. He tossed the toilet paper into the empty toilet and flushed before pulling his shirt sleeve down to his elbow.

He opened the stall door to see the surgeon who'd performed the spinal fusion washing his hands. Their eyes met in the mirror. Jerad smiled and moved toward the neighboring sink.

"Hey John. How are the kids?"

CHAPTER FIFTEEN

Malorie leaned against her apartment door after the detectives had left. *Lani was pregnant? She couldn't have been.* There was no way she wouldn't have told her. But she hadn't told her about her mystery date on Saturday night, so maybe they weren't as close as Malorie had thought.

Was that the real reason why Lani hadn't been drinking? When she thought about it, Lani had been wearing looser-fitting clothing lately. Malorie had thought maybe she'd put on a little weight from the stress of school. It happened.

She went to Lani's room and flicked on the lights. She stood in the doorway. Even though Lani was missing, it felt a little wrong to intrude on her privacy. But Lani's life might depend on it. She went through all the papers and notebooks on Lani's desk. It was all school related.

She looked through her messy closet and her dresser, but she found nothing but Lani's unorganized clothes. She spun around, trying to think of where else she could look. Her movement knocked a large textbook off the top edge of Lani's dresser.

When she picked it up, she noticed there was a small piece of paper tucked inside like a bookmark. She pulled it out. She held her breath when she recognized it as an ultrasound photo. It was dated last Friday, the day before Lani went missing. *Wu, Lani 22w 0d* was printed in the top right corner.

Malorie sat on the floor as she admired the tiny fetus. *Twenty-two weeks. Lani had been pregnant for over five months.* How could she have kept this from her? And how had she been too blind to notice?

There was a knock on her door. Maybe her uncle and Detective Stephenson had forgotten to ask her something. She tucked the black and white photo back into the textbook before going to answer it.

She was surprised to see Lani's ex-boyfriend standing outside her doorway instead of the detectives.

"Dante. Hi."

"I was here visiting some friends. I heard about Lani," he said. "Can I come in?"

In the four years he dated Lani, he'd never tried to get to know Malorie. Even when he'd come to their apartment, he would act like Malorie wasn't even there. Lani had been crushed when he'd broken up with her in May, but Malorie thought her roommate had probably dodged a bullet.

He was arrogant. She'd seen it even in class. He didn't give attention to anyone unless he was getting something in return.

She stepped aside to make room for him to pass through the doorway. "Sure."

He ran his hands through his dark, wavy hair as he walked through her apartment to their small living area. He took a seat in one of her chairs, wasting no time in making himself at home. She closed her apartment door.

VIABLE HOSTAGE

"I can't believe it," he said as Malorie moved toward the small living room. "Do you think it's just like the last time she did this or do you think something's really happened to her?"

Malorie sat on the couch opposite him. "Honestly, I think she's either being held against her will somewhere or she's—" She couldn't bring herself to say the word.

"Damn. That's so crazy."

Crazy? Malorie thought. He said it like he thought it was fascinating.

"Did you hear about the body that was found yesterday on Alki Beach? It was another EBU med student. The article I read said police are investigating whether there's a connection between her and Lani's disappearance. I mean, that's pretty crazy."

More like disturbing. Or terrifying, because it could mean Lani was dead. Malorie narrowed her eyes at Lani's ex-boyfriend. They'd broken up in May. It was now October. She counted the months in her head. Five. *Was Dante the father of her child? Did he know?*

Dante stood from his chair and moved around the coffee table. He sat next to her on the couch and placed his hand on her knee.

"It's really made me think, you know?"

Malorie scooted back until his hand slid off her leg.

"We never really got to know each other."

Because you never wanted to, Malorie thought.

"I realized lately that was a mistake."

Malorie hadn't noticed him slip his arm around the back of the couch. He leaned forward and pressed his mouth to hers. Malorie jerked back and stood from the couch.

"I think you should leave."

Dante reached for her hand. "Malorie, I—"

Malorie drew back her hand and turned for the door. She held it open while she waited for him to follow. He slowly walked across their apartment. He paused before moving through her doorway.

"This has been a tough week for both of us. But, trust me, if you knew the real Lani, you might not be so upset that's she's gone," he said.

Malorie's face flushed with anger. "Get out!"

Dante placed his hand on top of her shoulder. She slapped it away.

"Call me when you're ready to talk," he said.

Without a word, she slammed the door behind him. Her hands were shaking as she turned the lock on the door. *What an asshole.* It made her sick to think he was the father of Lani's child. What did he mean, *the real Lani?* Malorie knew the real Lani. Despite her flaws, she loved her. And she wouldn't be at peace until she knew what happened to her best friend.

She headed back into the living room. Seeing her radiology textbook on the kitchen table, she remembered her midterm tomorrow morning. She hadn't even started studying. She grabbed the textbook and her laptop off the table and brought them into the living room.

She sat on the couch, pushing away the disgusting memory of Dante at the lingering scent of his cologne. She tried to focus over the next couple hours, but she couldn't keep her mind on her studies. Her thoughts drifted between Lani, her baby, Dante, and Dr. Delaney.

She thought about what her uncle and Detective Stephenson had said about Dr. Delaney being in Spokane when Lani got into that car. It didn't make any sense. And, if he hadn't taken Lani, who had?

She grabbed her phone off the coffee table, remembering she needed to call Detective Stephenson about the ultrasound photo. It was late, but he needed to know. As she put the detective's number into her phone, Malorie prayed that Lani wasn't taken by the same person who'd taken Tina. And that her pregnancy wasn't the reason she'd been targeted. Detective Stephenson's voice tore her thoughts away from a horrifying image of her best friend when he answered on the second ring.

He didn't sound surprised when Malorie told him about finding the ultrasound photo. They didn't talk for long. He thanked her before hanging up.

After she got off the phone, Malorie caught herself staring blankly at her computer screen and textbook several times. Finally, she lay her head back on the end of the couch and closed her eyes. She was exhausted from her anxiety over Lani's disappearance and from barely sleeping the last two nights. She needed to rest her eyes for a few minutes and push her anxious thoughts aside. Then, she could focus on passing her exam.

Malorie squinted from the morning sunlight shining through her living room window when she awoke on the couch. Her textbook was opened across her chest. She sat up and rubbed her eyes. She was still wearing the same clothes she'd had on last night and realized she must've never woken up after she meant to close her eyes for only a few minutes. She reached for her phone on the coffee table and saw she had a missed call from her mom.

She was about to call her back but jumped off the couch when she saw the time. *9:05*. Her radiology midterm was at eight.

"No. Not again!"

And she was late for her nine o'clock class. She grabbed her bag and scrambled out of her apartment.

CHAPTER SIXTEEN

"I think I may have just found our main suspect in Lani's disappearance."

Stephenson spun around in his chair to face his partner. Pete had sent them Tina's official autopsy results that morning, which didn't give them much that they didn't already know. He had determined her cause of death to have been exsanguination through her uterine and abdominal incision.

The hospital gown Tina had worn belonged to Elliot Bay University Medical Center. But the hospital had no records of Tina ever being a patient. They hadn't found any evidence on Alki Beach that pointed to the identity of Tina's killer.

They'd also received Lani's medical records first thing that morning. They'd confirmed what Malorie had told Stephenson last night: Lani was twenty-two weeks pregnant.

"I'm still looking through her emails, but I stayed up late last night going through the data TESU extracted from Lani's phone," Adams said.

The Technical Electronic Support Unit was part of their Intelligence Unit and had offices on the same floor as the

Homicide Unit.

"According to her roommate, Malorie, Lani said she got a call from the guy who was supposed to pick her up from Harry's right before she left the bar. But the only call she received on Saturday was from Malorie. I went through Lani's text messages, and there wasn't really anything of note. Except, some texts between Lani and her brother, Tyler, where she asked him not to say anything to their parents. She didn't specify what it was about. He replied by saying, *It's not my problem. It's yours.* This was about two months ago. Lani never replied and there haven't been any texts between them since.

"I ran Tyler's name this morning and found that a car had just been registered in his name today. A 2019 silver Mercedes Roadster. It was purchased a week ago, which was why it hadn't come up when Tess ran Lani's family members through the database."

That was big news. Neither Lani's parents nor Tyler had mentioned he drove a silver Mercedes when they told them Lani was last seen getting into one.

Stephenson's desk phone rang before he could respond. He checked the caller ID and saw the call was from the front desk of the public entrance to the Police Headquarters building.

"Detective Stephenson."

"Hi, Detective. I've got a woman here who would like to speak with you and your partner about Dr. Jerad Delaney. She has information that she believes links him to the murder of the woman you found on Alki Beach yesterday."

Stephenson stood from his chair. Hopefully this would be something useful. "Thanks. I'll be right down."

"What's that?" Adams asked.

"A woman is downstairs asking to speak to us about Dr. Jerad Delaney. She thinks he killed Tina Lang."

"Hopefully it's not McKinnon's niece. Tess said she was pretty upset she didn't process the doctor's car."

"I don't think so. McKinnon and I spoke to her last night. We told her about Dr. Delaney's alibi for Saturday night. She can't argue with that. Plus, she didn't know Tina."

Adams stood and followed Stephenson out of the Homicide Unit. "Speaking of Tess, when is she coming back to Homicide?"

"Soon. I think the detective she's filling in for is returning from maternity leave in a few weeks."

They both knew the reason Tess had volunteered to transfer from Homicide to Missing Persons for a few months. And neither of them blamed her.

"Did she tell you they've set a date for her brother's murder trial?" Adams asked.

"No. But I haven't really had a chance to talk to her in the last few days." Stephenson felt guilty for not knowing. "Did you ever get a hold of the Bainbridge detective yesterday about the hand?"

"Yeah. It was pretty late when he called me back. As you probably already know, almost all unidentified human remains get sent to the University of North Texas Center for Human Identification. But, since their current processing time is over nine months, the Bainbridge detectives got approval to send the bones to a private laboratory in Salt Lake City. They're expecting DNA results any day." Adams turned for the door to the adjacent parking garage when Stephenson reached the elevator. "Let me know how it goes with the woman downstairs."

"Where are you going?"

"EBU. I'm going to see if I can get Tyler to come back here and have a chat."

Stephenson sat across from Dr. Althea Muna in the small interview room. Detective Amber Morgan from the Sex Crimes Unit sat to his right. After he learned what the doctor came to accuse Dr. Delaney of, he'd called the Sex Crimes Unit and invited one of their detectives to join them.

Amber had volunteered when she heard it was about Jerad Delaney. She'd told Stephenson before they entered the interview room that she'd been the one to arrest him for rape eight years earlier. She wasn't surprised to hear there had been another victim, and she'd been more than happy to come down and hear what Althea had to say.

"So, this happened two years ago?" he asked.

"Yes." Althea tucked her black shoulder-length hair behind her ear. "I was a fourth-year medical student at EBU."

"If a rape isn't reported within a year, the statute of limitations in Washington State gives us three years after the crime to prosecute," Amber said. "So, there's still time if you want to press charges."

"Can you tell us what happened?" Stephenson asked.

She nodded. Her eyes focused on the table between them. "He told me he wanted to speak to me after class about my midterm results. I had studied hard and felt like the exam had gone okay, but he made it sound like I had failed it."

She paused to take a sip from her water on the table. Her hand shook when she set down the paper cup.

"I've never told anyone this before."

"It's okay," Amber said. "You're doing great."

"He took me to his office and closed the door. It was afternoon. The lights were on in his office, but the blinds were closed. He told me to sit and he set two glasses and a bottle of bourbon on his desk. I started to feel uneasy, like maybe he hadn't brought me back to talk about my exam after all. But he told me I probably wanted to have a drink before we talked about my test results. I assumed I was about to get some very bad news. So, I took the drink. By the time I finished it, I could barely understand a word he was saying. The room was spinning. He asked if I wanted to lie down. I said yes.

"He helped me to the couch in his office. Just walking across the room made me feel like I was going to faint. I had no idea what was happening. I heard him lock his office door, and I knew something was wrong. But I was too weak to get up. I was aware of him reaching under my dress and pulling off my underwear, but I couldn't move. I was a prisoner in my own body. Then, he raped me."

Tears spilled down her cheeks onto the table.

"I wish I would've been unconscious so I wouldn't have to remember. But I didn't pass out until after he put his pants back on and left me alone on his couch. When I woke up hours later, it was dark. I was the only one left in the building. I found my underwear lying on the floor next to the couch."

"Why didn't you report it?" Amber asked. The detective's eyes weren't judging, rather trying to understand.

"I was dazed and in shock after it happened. I went back to my apartment and took a shower. I couldn't stand the smell of him on me. I wanted to wash it all away. I realized afterward that was a stupid thing to do. That I probably destroyed evidence that could've been used in a rape kit."

"But you still didn't get one?"

"No. I'd heard about the student he raped several years earlier. It went to trial. He got off. Dr. Delaney's attorneys made the woman look like a lying, attention-seeking cheat who'd accused her professor as a desperate measure to pass his class. They ripped her story apart. Made her look like a fool. After the trial, she flunked out. And I'm sure the school was thrilled to see her go.

"His wife is the president of the university. Dr. Delaney had already taken enough from me. I wasn't going to let him take my medical degree from me too. So, I never said a word. Until now."

The detectives waited in silence for her to continue.

"When I saw in the news that the body on Alki Beach was Tina Lang, I knew Dr. Delaney killed her. She's exactly his type. So is the other student who went missing over the weekend. Lani Wu. I take it you haven't found her body yet?"

"No," Stephenson said.

"He's progressed. Raping his students must not be enough for him anymore. Now he's killing them," Althea said.

Stephenson decided not to tell her that Jerad Delaney had an alibi for the night Lani went missing.

"If you're willing to press charges, I can make a probable cause arrest today for the rape," Amber said, using the tip of her finger to brush a short, blonde curl to the side of her forehead. "It will probably go to trial after he's formally charged. Would you be willing to accuse him in court?"

Althea wiped the tears away from her cheeks. "Yes. There's nothing more he can do to me now. I'm already a doctor. And I want the world to know what he did. I want justice for all the women he's raped…and killed."

Stephenson refrained from stating that his history of sexual assaults didn't necessarily make him guilty of murder. But he appreciated her sentiment. She did deserve justice. Along with all the other women he'd assaulted.

"Great," Amber said. "I'll get the paperwork drawn up. And I'll walk you out, unless there's anything else you'd like to tell us?"

She shook her head. "No. That's all."

"Thank you for coming in," Stephenson said as the three of them stood from their chairs. "And I'm very sorry for what's happened to you."

"Thank you."

Stephenson turned around to face her when he reached the doorway. "When we were in the elevator, did you say you'll be doing a fellowship in neonatology after your pediatric residency?"

"Yes."

"Did you spend time in a NICU during your residency?"

"Six months."

"Can I ask you something?"

"Sure." She dabbed the corner of her eye with a tissue she'd pulled from her purse.

"How many weeks does a fetus have to be to survive outside the womb when it's born?"

"Generally, we consider twenty-three to twenty-four weeks gestation to be the limits of viability. They don't often resuscitate infants less than twenty-three weeks due to the poor survival rates. The survival rates and outcomes for extremely premature infants have improved in recent years for babies born between twenty-three and twenty-four weeks, but not for infants born less than that."

"And what would be the survival rate for an extremely premature infant outside of a neonatal intensive care unit?"

"You mean one that was transferred to a NICU shortly after birth?"

"No. I mean one that was kept away from the hospital entirely."

"None. They wouldn't survive. Not that early."

Stephenson nodded. "Thank you."

He ran into Adams and Tyler when he stepped out into the hall.

"This is my partner, Detective Blake Stephenson," Adams said to Tyler as he led the med student into Interview Room Two. "You're going to love him. Don't be fooled by the pretty face. He's sharp as a tack."

Adams winked at his partner before directing Tyler to take a seat. Stephenson shook his head at Adams's stupid attempt at humor. He tried to smile.

"You want to join us?" Adams asked.

"Love to," Stephenson said.

Adams waited for Stephenson to take a seat before starting the interview.

Lani's brother wore designer jeans and a name brand zip-up hoodie. He tried to appear calm by folding his hands in his lap, but his left leg shook with a nervous tension.

"We really appreciate you coming here today, Tyler," Adams started.

"Of course," he said.

"I learned something this morning. And it was really puzzling, because when Detective Richards told you and your parents that Lani had been last seen in a silver two-door Mercedes on Saturday night, all three of you acted as

VIABLE HOSTAGE

if you had no idea whose car it could've been. But you drive a silver, two-door Mercedes, don't you? It was purchased last week and registered in your name only this morning."

Tyler glanced at Stephenson before meeting Adams's gaze. "I—we didn't think it was worth mentioning since I haven't seen her in over a week. Plus, at that time, we didn't really think she was missing."

"Where did you think she was?" Stephenson asked.

"Sleeping off a hangover in some random person's apartment. Like she did when she missed my college graduation last May."

"And what do you think now that she's been gone nearly seventy-two hours and we found the remains of another EBU med student on Alki Beach yesterday morning?"

"I think it's possible she's in trouble. But I'm still not totally convinced. Lani has always done what's best for Lani. Not caring about how she affects anyone else."

"So, you two didn't have a good relationship?"

Tyler stared at Stephenson for a moment before answering. "No."

"Last night, I came across some texts between you and your sister from late August," Adams said. "She asked you not to tell your parents. And you replied that it wasn't your problem. But hers. What were you referring to?"

"She was pregnant." Tyler shook his head. "Of course she was. Halfway through med school and she gets herself knocked up. We were spending a week with my parents at their weekend home on Whidbey Island when I found out. She was throwing up like three times a day. She'd been able to hide it from my parents but not me. She didn't deny it when I confronted her about it. She just begged me not to tell our parents."

Tyler pulled back the sleeve of his sweatshirt and adjusted his watch. Stephenson noticed it was a Rolex.

"When was the last time you saw Lani?" Adams asked.

"Wednesday. I saw her at the Health Sciences building on campus. We didn't speak."

"So, she's never been in your new car?" Stephenson asked.

Tyler looked between the detectives.

"Would you mind if our CSI team processed your Mercedes so we can clear you as a suspect?" Adams asked when Tyler didn't respond.

Tyler remained silent.

"Or do you have something to hide?" he added.

Tyler adjusted his Rolex again. "I saw her. Saturday night. I was driving back to my apartment and she was standing outside Harry's bar in the rain. She made such a big deal about how she'd 'changed' since last May. It pissed me off to see her hanging out at a bar, pregnant nonetheless, when she had a week of midterms coming up. So, I stopped and asked her to get in. I wanted to know what she was doing."

The two detectives avoided each other's gaze. Tyler had just confessed to being the last person to see Lani before she disappeared. And to lying about it before.

"She got in and then accused me of sending her threatening emails about blowing her secret. I told her I hadn't sent any emails, but I was mad she still hadn't told our parents about the baby. She was over five months along. People were going to start finding out. She was going to have to drop out of med school. Our parents deserved to know. But Lani never thought about anyone but herself." He ran a hand through his straight black hair. "We were a few blocks from the bar when she told me to stop the car. She got out and I drove away. I haven't seen her since."

"Why did she think you sent the emails? Did they come from your account?" Adams asked.

"She said she didn't recognize the email address but assumed they were from me since I was the only person who knew about her pregnancy."

"Why didn't you say anything before? About seeing her and about the emails?"

"When she didn't show up to my mom's award ceremony, I figured she'd just forgotten about it. Or done something stupid the night before. I didn't want to have to explain what we'd argued about."

"And you didn't think to say anything after her roommate filed a missing persons report and you were questioned by a detective?" Stephenson asked.

He shrugged his shoulders. "Didn't seem like it made any difference. She was still alive when she got out of my car."

"We could charge you for obstruction of justice for lying to a police officer, do you know that?" Adams asked.

Tyler stood from his chair. "I didn't do anything! I didn't think it mattered, okay?" He threw up his hands.

"Would you allow us to process your car? It would help us eliminate you as a suspect in your sister's disappearance."

"Fine." Tyler swiped his hand through the air. "Go ahead."

"Could you give us your keys?" Adams asked.

Tyler tossed them onto the table in front of Stephenson.

Stephenson took the keys from the table and turned to his partner. "I'll let CSI know."

"Come on," Adams said to Tyler. "I'll give you a ride

back to EBU."

Tyler followed the detectives out of the interview room without another word.

Adams nearly ran into his homicide sergeant when he stepped into the hallway.

"You better get downstairs," McKinnon said. "I just got a call from the front desk. Tyler's father is in the lobby making a big scene about his son being questioned without an attorney."

Stephenson turned to his partner. "How did he know we were questioning him?"

"I texted him on the way here," Tyler said from the doorway of the interview room.

"Let's go." Adams started to lead Tyler out of the Homicide Unit.

"I'll come with you," Stephenson said. "You might need my muscle."

Adams couldn't suppress a laugh at his partner's comment while they waited for the elevator. He eyed Stephenson's lean frame. Even through his suit, it was obvious Adams had the build of a bodybuilder.

When the elevator reached the first floor, the detectives were all business. They escorted Tyler through the locked glass doors to the lobby of the Police Headquarters.

They heard Dr. Jian Wu's shouting as they entered the lobby. "How dare they question my son without a lawyer!"

His face was pressed against the glass that separated him from the officer behind the front desk. He turned in their direction as the three of them entered the lobby. He wore surgical scrubs with no coat. He glared at the detectives.

"What the hell are you doing questioning my son? And without an attorney? He has rights! I'll sue if you coerced him into telling you what you wanted to hear." His finger was pointed high at Adams's face.

Tyler moved across the lobby and stood next to his father. He stared at the ground, like a child being scolded.

"He never asked for an attorney. He came here of his own free will," Adams said. "We could have you both charged with obstruction of justice for lying about Tyler owning a silver Mercedes when you were questioned by Detective Richards."

Tyler's father scoffed. "Tyler had already told us he hadn't seen Lani since last week. So it wasn't worth mentioning. We didn't want the detective wasting her time suspecting Tyler if there really was someone out there who'd taken Lani."

His voice broke. His mouth quivered as he brought a hand to his face. "We didn't think at the time that she was really missing."

Tyler put a hand on his father's shoulder, but his dad shook it away. He wiped the tears from his eyes and stepped toward the detectives. Adams lifted his hand and rested it on his firearm.

Dr. Wu stopped a few inches from their faces. He stared at Adams through his watery eyes. "Just find my daughter. Before it's too late."

Stephenson and Adams watched him storm out of the building with his son following close behind.

CHAPTER SEVENTEEN

Malorie sat in the back of the lecture hall of Dr. Delaney's anesthesiology class, unable to focus on anything he said. She was disgusted at the sight of him. She noticed his belly hung slightly over his belt through his tucked-in button-up shirt. He placed a hand over his mouth and stifled a yawn as his presentation switched to a new screen.

"Excuse me," he said.

Malorie tried not to think about why he might be so tired. He was a rapist, but she hoped he wasn't a killer.

Her attention moved to Dante sitting in his usual seat in the front row. He was almost as disgusting as their professor. He'd even had the nerve to smile at her that morning despite his behavior the night before.

And, if all of that wasn't enough, she now had other problems. She was retaking Dr. Delany's midterm after his class, but she still had to see if she could retake the other midterm she'd missed that morning. She hadn't been able to speak with her radiology professor yet about missing the exam, and she figured it would be best to speak with the Dean of Medicine to explain her absences, as well.

She'd sent his office an email that morning requesting a meeting, and he'd agreed to see her later that afternoon. She could only hope he would be understanding.

She tore her eyes away from the back of Dante's head at the sound of the door to the lecture hall opening. Dr. Delaney paused mid-sentence as a university security guard led Detective Stephenson and a woman who Malorie didn't recognize into the lecture hall. They both wore suits, and the woman had short blonde curls. They marched directly toward Dr. Delaney. The woman pulled a pair of handcuffs out of her jacket pocket and exposed a badge on her hip with the other hand. Stephenson looked to have one hand on his holstered firearm, and the other exposing his badge.

Stephenson's square jaw and dark blue eyes were visible even from across the room. Malorie saw for the first time how attractive he was. She must've been too upset over Lani to notice when he'd come to her apartment with her uncle Wade.

"He's hot," Malorie heard the student behind her whisper.

"Jerad Delaney," the woman said loudly enough for the class to hear as she approached him, "you are under arrest for the rape of Althea Muna." She read him his Miranda Rights as she placed his hands in the cuffs behind his back.

Another student must've come forward, Malorie thought. She wondered if their reason had anything to do with the recent news about Tina and Lani. If the Seattle police knew he was guilty of this, hopefully that meant they were investigating him for Lani's disappearance-even though he supposedly had an alibi.

A few students pulled out their phones and took video of the arrest. Stephenson stood between the doctor and the door. The security guard held the door open for them as the two detectives led the professor out of the lecture hall. Dr. Delaney's eyes scanned the class as he was escorted across the room. They stopped when he found Malorie. His eyes narrowed, and he didn't break eye contact until he was led out the door.

"Were you also meeting with a detective when you missed this morning's midterm?"

The Dean of Medicine's mouth had been fixed in a permanent frown ever since Malorie had entered his large office.

"Well, no. Not this morning. But they did visit my apartment last night. I haven't gotten much sleep since Lani went missing. I meant to close my eyes for only a few minutes last night and forgot to set an alarm. I woke up and saw that I'd slept through the exam."

"I understand that you're worried about Lani."

From his blank expression, Malorie didn't think he understood at all.

"But," he went on, "this isn't the first time Lani has disappeared like this, as I'm sure you know."

"But-"

The Dean held up his hand. "Lani is lucky to still be in the medicine program. Given her history, I don't think she's been missing long enough for anyone to jump to conclusions."

Jump to conclusions? Had he really just said that when another student's decayed remains had washed ashore yesterday morning? And when one of their professors had just been arrested for rape for the second time?

Malorie didn't know what to say.

"Since you have a nearly perfect GPA and no history of skipping class or missing exams, I'll allow you to re-take both of these midterms this afternoon. I'm not going to allow you extra time for studying, as that wouldn't be fair to the rest of the students. I'll see if Dr. Green can proctor you in the Cascade Lecture Hall. If you don't pass, or if you miss any more exams, I'll have no choice but to place you on academic probation." The Dean stood from his chair, indicating their meeting was over. "If you'll excuse me, I have some things to take care of in the wake of Dr. Delaney's arrest."

"Thank you," she heard herself say before leaving his office. She checked the time on her phone as she walked down the hall of faculty offices. *3:30*.

She'd hardly studied for her radiology midterm last night before falling asleep. She didn't have enough time to go back to her apartment, so she decided to go sit outside the Cascade Lecture Hall and cram what she could before her exams. She *had* to pass them. Her lifelong dream of becoming a doctor might depend on it.

CHAPTER EIGHTEEN

The man leaned back against the driver seat headrest, his neck muscles tense from the strain of the last few days. He hadn't gotten much sleep the last three nights due to capturing Lani, acting normal around his neighbors, and keeping up his presence at the university. Not to mention almost losing his primary research subject over the weekend. But, with Tina's baby stabilized and Lani safely contained, he was looking forward to a good night's sleep that evening.

He'd been surprised to see that Tina's body had washed ashore on Alki Beach the previous morning. He'd known there was a chance a part of her remains would surface, but he'd been hopeful they never would. While it was nice his research subject had made the headlines, he didn't like the fact that her remains were in the hands of a Seattle Medical Examiner. Although, he was certain an ME wouldn't find anything that could be traced back to him.

Nothing had come of Gretchen's skeletal hand being found by a crabber off Bainbridge Island in July. Bainbridge Police still didn't know who it belonged to. Although, with current DNA technology, it probably wouldn't be long before they did. While sawing Gretchen's remains into pieces and placing them into garbage bags before he dumped them into the Sound seemed like a good idea at the time, he realized there would've been less chance of a part of her coming to the surface if he'd left her in one piece.

The late afternoon sun peeked through the clouds. He drove around the north side of Lake Union, passing by several marinas. He'd been keeping a close eye on Tina's baby and Lani throughout the day, thanks to the live camera feeds on his phone.

Lani had been dozing on and off, uselessly attempting to free herself from the handcuffs in between her rest. Her attempts at escape were so pitiful, it almost made him smile. Tina's baby's hemodynamic monitoring remained stable, but she was due for an antibiotic to finish out the course he'd started on the weekend. While he could check on them anytime from his phone, he felt better when he checked on them in person. He'd worked too hard and risked too much to lose either of his research subjects.

The research he was conducting wasn't even his own idea. Similar testing had been done on fetal lambs placed in synthetic uterine-like environments. Their research concluded with promising results of improving outcomes for extremely premature fetuses. However, due to ethical restraints, no further research had been conducted on human test subjects. He was furious after reading the article on the fetal lamb research, knowing that human testing might never be done. The study had proven effective, but mankind was left unable to benefit. Until something changed. Until someone pioneered and stopped ethical standards from holding back the world from an elevated existence. With extreme prematurity being the leading cause of neonatal morbidity and mortality in developed countries, he found these ethical limitations on research to be ludicrous and unethical in themselves.

If it weren't for all the ethical restrictions on medical research, he could be living in a world free of cancer, among many other diseases. What ever happened to sacrificing the few to save the many?

He'd always known he was exceptional, even if his genius was hidden in his family's shadow of high achievements. The lake came in and out of his view as he drove past Gas Works park. He tapped his finger against the steering wheel. With Tina's baby out of the woods and Lani quietly contained on the houseboat, there was only one threat to his achievements. *Malorie.*

He hadn't factored in her uncle being a sergeant for Seattle Homicide. His options were limited, however, since he needed pregnant women of a specific gestation who, he hoped, wouldn't be missed too greatly. He wondered what he should do if she continued to be a problem.

He pulled the Mercedes into the parking area adjacent to a small houseboat community. He wasn't going to allow his life to be a waste. He was destined to be more than someone who simply took up space, consumed oxygen, and contributed to the further devastation of the planet until he died. And, no one was going to stand in his way of leaving his mark on humanity.

So, he had taken it upon himself to do what was necessary to make a medical breakthrough. To make the world a better place. He would be famous for it, but that didn't matter.

He would, of course, wait to publish his research until he was out of the country, safely established in South

America. Away from the American justice system and in a place where there was lots of work for doctors on the black market. He'd find a way to conduct further research. Studies the world refused to do. He doubted he would have any trouble finding funding once his medical breakthroughs became world famous, even if his studies didn't meet ethical standards. He would be known for curing countless diseases, even eradicating cancer in his lifetime.

CHAPTER NINETEEN

"I spoke with Tyler's roommate," Adams said.

Stephenson turned in his desk chair to face his partner.

"He confirmed that Tyler came home to their apartment at eight-thirty on Saturday night and stayed until he went to his mother's award ceremony the next day. CSI is still processing his car, so we'll see if that turns up anything."

The city outside was dark; the other two detectives from their squad had gone home for the day. McKinnon was still in his office.

Both detectives looked up as Detective Morgan from the Sex Crimes Unit stepped into their cubicle.

"I brought Jerad Delaney into Interview One so you can question him before I book him into jail for the night," she said.

Stephenson stood from his chair. "Thanks."

"Jerad Delaney? What are you questioning him about? We've confirmed his alibi for the night Lani went missing," Adams said.

"But not for Tina's. I know he was in Spokane Saturday night, but something about him is bugging me."

"Like that he's a rapist?" Adams asked.

"I feel like he knows more than what he's telling us."

Adams shrugged his shoulders and turned back to his desk. "Yeah, he's probably guilty of a lot more rapes than just two."

Stephenson ignored his partner and followed Detective Morgan down the hall. He stopped when his girlfriend and fellow homicide detective, Tess, stepped out of her cubicle in front of him. Her purse was slung over her shoulder and her eyes looked red from crying.

"Are you okay?" he asked.

Detective Morgan turned and waited for him to follow.

"Yeah, I'm fine." She brushed past him. "I'll see you tomorrow."

"Sorry, just a second," he said to the sex crimes detective.

"Tess, wait!"

She kept walking, picking up her pace as she neared the door to the seventh-floor parking lot adjacent to their offices.

Stephenson grabbed her arm. "What's wrong?"

She pulled her arm away from him. "Nothing. I can't do this here."

He let her go. "I'll call you tonight," he said before she walked through the door.

He figured her brother's upcoming murder trial was the reason behind her emotions. It had been almost four months since Chris's death, and Tess hadn't been the same since it happened.

Stephenson turned in Detective's Morgan's direction. "Sorry, let's go."

Jerad Delaney was handcuffed to the interview table with a well-dressed defense attorney at his side.

VIABLE HOSTAGE

Stephenson introduced himself and took a seat across from them. Detective Morgan watched from the one-way mirrored glass in the adjoining room.

"I'd like to ask you a few questions about your student, Tina Lang, whose partial remains were found on Alki Beach yesterday morning."

Jerad's attorney turned to his client. "You look at me before you answer."

Jerad nodded.

"Tina Lang was a student of yours, right?"

Jerad glanced at his attorney, who nodded his approval of the question.

"Yes."

"And what was your relationship with Tina?"

"Don't answer that," the attorney said.

"I was her professor. She was my student," Jerad said.

Stephenson watched his attorney roll his eyes in frustration.

"Nothing more?" Stephenson pressed.

Jerad's attorney placed the back of his hand on Jerad's chest. "*Don't* answer that." He turned to Stephenson. "My client has already answered your question. He was her professor. She was his student."

"And where were you on the evening of August fifteenth?"

"I don't know. That was almost three months ago."

Stephenson waited in silence to see if he would elaborate.

"I was probably working at the hospital," Jerad said after a minute.

"I'll see if I can confirm that."

"My client has had a very long day." Jerad's attorney

smoothed the front of his bright-colored tie. "I think that's enough."

Jerad stared at the cuffs on his wrists.

"Fine." Stephenson pushed back his chair. "I'll let Detective Morgan know you're ready for her."

"Do you know what's wrong with Tess?" Stephenson asked his partner when he got back to his desk.

Adams was the lead investigator of her brother's homicide. If she was upset about his upcoming trial, Adams probably knew why.

"Her brother's killer has just entered a plea of not guilty by reason of insanity."

"*What?* That's ridiculous. His death was planned. Premeditated."

"*We* know that. Hopefully a jury will see that too," Adams said.

No wonder Tess was so upset, Stephenson thought.

"I found the emails to Lani that Tyler told us about. The ones she'd thought he sent. I printed them off." Adams handed Stephenson a few sheets of paper.

"The sender's name comes up as 'Your Friend', and there's no actual name associated with the email account. The sender's email has only been accessed by one IP address, and we've traced it to a shared-access hospital computer at EBU Medical Center."

Stephenson flipped through the pages. The emails were short. The last one to Lani stated they would pick her up in front of Harry's at eight p.m. last Saturday night. Lani lied to her roommate about getting a call from the person who was picking her up, but she *did* have plans to meet someone.

VIABLE HOSTAGE

"The computer is on a surgical floor," Adams continued. "According to the person I spoke with at the hospital, nurses, doctors, and even medical students would have access to it."

"So, that would include both Dr. Delaney and Tyler," Stephenson thought aloud. He handed the printed emails back to Adams. "Did Tina Lang receive any emails from this address?"

"No. Her phone was never found, but we haven't found anything useful from her cell records or emails. Did you learn anything more from questioning Jerad?"

Stephenson ran his palm down the back of his short blond hair. "Not really. He says he was working at the hospital the night Tina Lang went missing."

Stephenson checked his watch. It was after eight. He'd have to wait until business hours tomorrow to confirm the doctor's alibi with EBU Medical Center. He tapped his fingers on his desk as he thought about the doctor.

"Can you stop tapping like that?" Adams asked. "You're going to make me go crazy."

Stephenson turned to his partner. "We have Dr. Delaney on security footage at his hotel in Spokane last weekend, but are we sure he took his Mercedes?"

"I didn't request any footage from the parking garage."

"What if Lani *did* get picked up in his Mercedes Saturday night? Only Jerad wasn't the one driving it?"

CHAPTER TWENTY

Malorie pulled her hooded sweatshirt over her head as she left the EBU campus library. A light rain fell from the sky that had grown dark while she'd studied. Her third midterm was tomorrow, and, after today's meeting with the Dean, she couldn't afford anything less than an A.

She'd taken the two midterms she'd missed that afternoon, back-to-back. After barely studying for her radiology midterm, she found herself guessing on several questions. She could only pray she got enough right to pass the exam. She'd hoped the library would help her focus on tomorrow's midterm instead of Lani, but her thoughts still kept drifting back to her roommate and her unborn child for most of the evening.

She hadn't spoken to Lani's parents about her pregnancy, but she wondered if the young detective had told them. She felt it wasn't her place to say anything, at least not yet. Especially when they hadn't even expressed concern over her disappearance on the weekend.

Malorie stepped off the curb onto the main campus street when the blare of a car horn caused her to jump back onto the sidewalk. She turned to see an SUV come to a hard stop inches from where she had stepped. The vehicle seemed to come out of nowhere. A middle-aged woman glared at her from behind the wheel. She looked familiar.

"Sorry," Malorie said, though every window in the SUV was rolled up tight. She took a deep breath, wondering how she could've been so careless.

The woman moved her cold stare to the road and accelerated without allowing Malorie to cross. The truck sprayed water onto Malorie's jeans from a puddle in the street. After she watched the SUV speed away, Malorie checked for cars before stepping back into the street. She crossed the road and remembered where she had seen the woman before. She was Carolyn Delaney. The President of EBU. And Jerad Delaney's wife.

From their encounter, Malorie didn't like her any more than she did her rapist husband. *And what was she doing at the university so late? Especially on the day of her husband's arrest.* It was past eleven o'clock at night.

Her phone rang and Malorie saw it was her mom. With all that had happened that day, she'd forgotten to return her call.

"Hi, Mom."

"Hi, sweetheart. Are you okay? I saw in the news about Lani. I'm so sorry."

"Yeah. I should've called. I'm sorry. I feel like the days have run into each other since she went missing."

"I talked to your uncle today. He assured me they're doing everything they can to find her. I know it must be incredibly hard, but I want you to try and stay positive. Are you doing okay?"

Malorie decided not to tell her about missing her midterms. Her dad was a high school teacher and her mom was a nurse. They both worked hard to help Malorie through med school. She felt guilty hearing her mother's voice when she was on the brink of academic probation, knowing how much her parents sacrificed to put her through school.

"I'm just worried about her. I have a bad feeling, Mom. Did you see in the news about the body they found yesterday on Alki Beach?"

There was a pause before her mother answered. "I did."

Malorie heard voices in the background.

"I'm sorry, sweetheart, but I have to go. I'm at work. I just wanted to make sure you were okay and let you know that I'm here for you."

She was surprised to hear that her mom was at work at that time of night. "Thanks, Mom. I didn't think you did nightshifts anymore."

"I don't usually, but this is an overtime."

To pay for my school. Malorie was flooded with guilt.

"I love you. Please call me if you need to talk. Or if you have any news about Lani."

"I will. I love you too."

Malorie tucked her phone into her jeans pocket as a group of students who looked to be undergrads passed by her in an array of ridiculous costumes. She remembered it was the night before Halloween. A couple of them burst out in laughter at something another had said. Malorie envied their lightheartedness as she watched them turn toward a dormitory building.

Malorie took a shortcut to her apartment and cut through a large lawn in the middle of the campus. The area was not well lit, but she could see well enough from the full moon that peeked through the clouds of the night sky.

She'd developed a new anxiety since Dr. Delaney's arrest. If he *had* taken Lani, and she was still alive, what would happen to her while he was in jail? Was she going without food? Without water? She'd taken a study break to check the news and saw that his bail hearing was set for tomorrow afternoon. She was irritated to see that there was no mention of him being linked to Tina's murder or Lani's disappearance.

She was still a few blocks from her apartment when she heard footsteps on the wet grass right behind her. They seemed to come out of nowhere. She felt a hand on her shoulder before she could turn around. She screamed.

"Whoa. It's just me. Luke."

Malorie spun around, knocking his hand away from her body. Her faced flushed in the dark field as she recognized her gorgeous classmate. She let out a deep breath.

"Sorry. I was thinking about Lani."

"I didn't mean to sneak up on you like that," he said. "You dropped these. I thought you might want them."

He held a stack of the *Missing* posters she'd made for Lani that were now damp from the rain.

"Thank you." She took them from his hands. She moved to unzip her book bag and saw she'd forgotten to zip it closed.

"I left the library just after you. They were lying in a pile outside the entrance. I called your name, but you must not have heard me."

She hadn't noticed him in the library, but it was a big place.

"You and Lani seemed kind of inseparable. You must be really worried about her."

She tucked the posters into her bag, making sure to zip

it closed this time. "I am."

"You live on campus?" he asked.

"Yeah, my building is just up ahead. What about you?"

"No, I live about twenty minutes away, depending on traffic. But I'll walk with you. Try and make up for scaring you like that."

Malorie smiled. She could use a distraction. Especially a drop-dead gorgeous one. "No, that wasn't your fault. I just can't stop thinking about Lani."

"I saw the news about Tina, the student who went missing a few months back. That's so awful. Did you know her?"

Malorie shook her head. "No."

An awkward silence passed between them.

"Sorry, I'm sure that's the last thing you need to be thinking about," Luke said. "Are you ready for the midterm tomorrow?"

"I hope so."

They passed through a small parking lot next to her apartment building.

"I haven't been able to concentrate very well though since Lani went missing."

"I bet. But I'm sure you'll do fine."

They stopped in front of the entrance to her apartment. Seeing him in the light, he was even more attractive than she had remembered. The rain had made his light brown hair look a few shades darker.

"I still have a little more studying to do tonight," he said. "But I couldn't sit in that library any longer."

"Do you want to come up and study for a bit in my apartment?" she asked as she looked into his hazel eyes.

"I should probably get home. It's late. I do better

studying early in the morning, anyway. But thanks."

"Okay. Sure. I guess I'll see you tomorrow?"

"See you then. Good luck on the midterm."

"Thanks. You too."

Malorie watched his tall, athletic form walk toward the parking lot. She let herself into her building, feeling stupid for inviting him up to her apartment. *He was just being nice,* she thought.

As she rode the elevator to the fifth floor, she was overcome with guilt for inviting a guy to her apartment when Lani and her unborn child were held captive against their will somewhere…or dead.

CHAPTER TWENTY-ONE

Wade came in through the garage, being careful to close the door quietly behind him. It was late, and he assumed Elle had already gone to bed. He'd barely seen her in the last two days. She was still asleep when he got called to Alki Beach early Monday morning to be the sergeant on-scene, and she'd been in bed when he'd gotten home last night at nearly eleven. He'd only seen her briefly that morning before work.

The door was open to their bedroom, but the light was off. He paused in the doorway. Elle lay on her side in their bed, her dark hair splayed across her pillow. He moved down the hall to their baby's room. He flicked on the light.

He saw Elle had finished putting the room together. There were navy blue polka-dotted sheets on the crib, books on the bookshelves, and stuffed animals neatly arranged on the window seat. Wade leaned against the door frame. At forty-six, he had long ago accepted that he would never have children. Before he met Elle, his life had been his work. He had spent much of his career obsessing over catching the Seattle Slasher, the infamous serial killer whose crimes plagued the Seattle area for over ten years.

When Wade's partner and best friend was shot and killed

during an arrest nearly eight years ago, he immersed himself even deeper into his homicide cases. He also drank heavily to numb the pain of his best friend's death, only to admit he was an alcoholic and seek help after he'd driven nearly everyone in his life away.

It wasn't just the grief of Cody's death that led him down a self-destructive path. It was the guilt that his decision not to involve SWAT in their arrest had cost Cody his life. It was something he'd learned to live with, and something he knew he'd never get over.

He wished Cody was alive to see his life now. How much he'd changed for the better over the last few years. Cody was always helping Wade become a better person, and his positive influence on Wade's life hadn't stopped when he died.

He'd been sober now for almost two years, about the same time he'd known Elle. He would've been sober for more than three years if he hadn't relapsed. Wade had returned to drinking when a spree of Seattle Slasher killings, including the murder of a detective from Wade's own squad, occurred one year after Wade had watched the Slasher die by lethal injection.

He'd worked hard to find balance in his life over the last two years. Sobriety, for him, was still a daily struggle. It had gotten easier the longer he stayed sober, but there were still times he wrestled with his desire to drink. He looked around at the beautiful nursery Elle had created for their son and worried he might not have what it took to be the father he wanted to be to his child.

Elle's voice tore him from his thoughts. "Do you like it?" She tucked her arm around his waist and rested her head on his shoulder.

VIABLE HOSTAGE

"I love it. Sorry, I didn't mean to wake you."

She stifled a yawn. "It's okay. Any news on Malorie's roommate?"

He pulled her closer. "Not really."

"You okay?" she asked.

"Things aren't looking good for Lani. If she was taken by the same person who killed Tina Lang, the student whose body we found yesterday morning, she's likely dead already."

They stood in silence for a moment, looking at the empty nursery. "There's nothing more you can do tonight, is there?" Elle asked.

"No."

"Then come to bed. You need some sleep."

Elle ran her hand down his back before turning for their room. Wade looked into his son's room for a moment longer before turning off the light.

CHAPTER TWENTY-TWO

The lights were on when Malorie opened the door to her apartment. Had she left them on? She couldn't remember.

She set her bag on the kitchen table and looked around the apartment. Something was off, but she wasn't sure what. There was a faint smell she didn't recognize. Nothing appeared out of place, but she had a creeping feeling someone had been inside her apartment.

She went to Lani's room and turned on the light. It was the same mess it always was. She crossed the hall and stood in the doorway to her own room. It was perfectly neat. Her bed was still made from yesterday morning, since she'd slept on the couch the night before.

She felt a chill when she returned to the living room. Her eyes moved toward their large window and the rain that spilled onto the floor under the opened windowpane. She moved across the room and pulled the window shut. She looked down at the fast-moving traffic five stories below.

Like the lights in the apartment, she couldn't remember opening the window. But she *did* open it from time to time. And she hadn't exactly been clear minded since Lani disappeared. Still, she wondered if she should call her uncle.

Although she couldn't waste his time when she wasn't even sure she hadn't opened it herself.

She turned from the window and scanned the apartment's main living space. It didn't leave many places for an intruder to hide. She was sure she was alone. Plus, being on the fifth floor, there was no way someone could've gotten in through the open window. Maybe she was growing paranoid from her lack of sleep. If she wanted to pass her midterm tomorrow, she needed to get some rest.

Malorie turned off the living room lights before heading to her room. She changed into sweats and crawled into bed. After two hours, she found herself staring at the ceiling, unable to will herself to fall asleep. She rolled over and checked the time on her phone. It was almost two a.m.

She threw back her covers and crossed the hall to Lani's room. She climbed into her roommate's unmade bed and lay her head atop Lani's pillow. When she smelled the familiar scent of Lani's perfume, she smiled.

Malorie turned on the lamp on Lani's bedside table and opened the textbook that lay on the nightstand. She pulled out the ultrasound photo and rolled onto her back. She traced her finger across the tiny form. Barely noticing the tears that escaped down her cheeks, she set the ultrasound photo back on the nightstand before turning out the light. She continued to think about her fun-loving friend until she was finally overcome by sleep.

There was something evil in the way he had looked at her. He was dangerous. Psychotic. Malorie could see it in his eyes. Those cold, dark eyes. He was chasing her.

Malorie ran faster, with so much adrenaline she didn't

feel the ache in her legs or the burn in her lungs as she gasped for air. She could feel him getting closer. Hear the sound of his boots scrape against the pavement behind her. *He's going to kill me.*

She felt him close in behind her. A sharp pain ripped through her arm as he grabbed her and drew her close to him with tremendous strength. Malorie opened her mouth to scream as she was awakened by the sound of her alarm.

She wasn't being chased. She was in Lani's room. She sat up in her roommate's bed, sweating through her t-shirt and breathing hard.

She silenced her alarm, flooded simultaneously with relief that it was just a dream and the familiar dread that her best friend was missing and possibly never coming back.

CHAPTER TWENTY-THREE

Stephenson took a seat across the table from Jerad Delaney in the same interview room where they had met the day before. Jerad's attorney did not look happy to see him. Stephenson tried not to stare at the attorney's neck fat that hung over the collar of his periwinkle shirt.

Stephenson fixed his gaze on the anesthesiologist. His one night in jail seemed to have taken a significant toll on him. Dark circles were evident under his bloodshot eyes. Jerad's forehead was beading with sweat, despite the cool temperature of the interview room.

Stephenson slid a photo across the table of Jerad getting into his wife's Audi A4 in the parking garage of his Spokane hotel. Although the hotel had sent Stephenson the security footage at ten o'clock the night before, it had taken him until two a.m. to find what he was looking for.

"I'd like you to see the date and time on this image." He pointed to the time stamp on the top right corner. "You know lying to the police is a felony, right? It's called obstruction of justice. If not, I'm sure your attorney can explain it to you."

Stephenson watched the defense attorney's frown

deepen.

"No one specifically asked me if I took my Mercedes last weekend," Jerad said.

"So who had access to your Mercedes while you were gone? Your wife?"

Jerad looked at his attorney, who nodded for him to answer. Jerad waited a moment before responding.

"Yes."

"And would you give us permission to search your Mercedes?"

"Not without a warrant," his attorney said before Jerad could answer.

"Fine. We'll request one." Stephenson turned to the professor. "Do you know where I might find your wife this morning?"

"I'm sure she's at work. At the university."

"Great." Stephenson tapped his hand on top of the interview table before getting up. He looked back at Jerad when he reached the door. "Anything else you'd like to tell me before I go?"

Jerad opened his mouth but quickly closed it. "No."

Adams hung up his desk phone and turned to Stephenson. "CSI has finished processing Tyler's Mercedes. They found Lani's fingerprints on the interior and exterior handles of the passenger door. But no blood, no hair, and no evidence of foul play anywhere else in the car. Being brand new, it was pretty spotless."

"That matches his story that she got into his car on Saturday night. Did he know Tina Lang?"

"Not that I can tell. I asked him that when I brought him

here yesterday morning, and he said no. There isn't any contact between them from Tina's phone records or her emails. Did you already go to EBU and question Delaney's wife?"

Stephenson shook his head. "I went to the courthouse to see if I could get a search warrant for his Mercedes before I spoke with her, but the judge denied it. She didn't think there was enough cause. I'm going to head to EBU soon and see what Jerad's wife has to say about having his Mercedes the night Lani went missing. I would say she has some motive, if her husband was raping his students. Maybe she took them out of jealousy."

"Yeah, but what about Tina's baby being cut out of her? Do you think Jerad's wife thought they were pregnant with his children? And that the president of EBU murdered Tina by cutting out her unborn child? And that she plans to do the same to Lani?"

"I don't know what to think. But we can't rule her out just because she's the president of EBU. I'm also going to see if I can talk to Lani's ex-boyfriend while I'm there, Dante. He's also a med student at the university. According to Wade's niece, they dated for four years, and he broke up with her last May. Four years is a long time. He might also be the father of her child. Although, he has a Ford Focus registered in his name, not a Mercedes."

McKinnon stepped into the middle of their cubicle. "Where are you two at with Tina and Lani's cases?"

Adams and Stephenson took turns bringing their sergeant up to speed with the investigation.

"Can you print me out copies of those emails to Lani from the unknown sender?" McKinnon asked. "I'll show them to Malorie and see if she has any idea who they might be from."

"Good idea," Adams said.

"I have a missing person who might be connected to Tina Lang and Lani Wu," Tess said from the edge of their cubicle.

She entered the small space and held out a thin case file toward Stephenson. He took it from her and flipped through the file as she continued.

"I've been going through some missing persons reports that were filed before I moved over from Homicide." She nodded at the file in Stephenson's hands. "Her name is Gretchen Hogan. She's thirty-two and worked as a pharmacy technician at the EBU Medical Center. She was last seen leaving the hospital after her shift on the thirtieth of May. She'd been missing for over a week before a coworker filed the missing persons report."

"There's not much here," Stephenson said.

"No, there's not. But there wasn't much to go on in Tina and Lani's reports either. She's estranged from most of her family, and most of them live on the east coast. Her coworker is the only person who's shown any concern over her disappearance."

Stephenson closed the thin folder. "She's Caucasian, and she wasn't a medical student at EBU. What makes you think her disappearance is related to Tina and Lani's?"

"When she went missing, she was five months pregnant."

Stephenson and Adams exchanged a look. Adams stretched out his hand and Stephenson gave him the file.

"Excuse me, Sergeant," Tess said from the edge of their cubicle. "Can I speak to you for a minute when you have time?"

VIABLE HOSTAGE

"Sure," he said. "You want to come into my office?"

"Yes, that would be great," she said.

"I'll print off those emails and bring them to you," Adams said to McKinnon.

"Thanks, Adams."

Tess followed the homicide sergeant through their cubicle on the way to his office. Stephenson wondered what she wanted to speak to him about. He and Adams had updated her that morning about where they were with Tina and Lani's cases, and Stephenson knew her well enough to know she was hurting. Even at work, he could see it in her face.

They had spoken last night on the phone, and, while Tess had assured him she was coping with Chris's killer pleading not guilty, he wasn't convinced. He was worried about her. He knew from his experience as a homicide detective that once the trial started, things would only get harder.

CHAPTER TWENTY-FOUR

Malorie scrolled through the local news on her phone as she waited for Lani's mom in a downtown Starbucks. The coffee shop was next door to the large hospital where Lani's mom served as the Medical Director. The place was busy for a weekday afternoon. A long line consisted of medical professionals in scrubs waiting to load up on caffeine before starting their shifts at the neighboring hospital.

Malorie hadn't been surprised to get a voicemail that morning from Tatiana asking to meet with her that afternoon. She assumed that by now the detectives would have told Lani's parents about her pregnancy. She brought along Lani's ultrasound photo to give to her mother.

Tatiana hadn't sounded her usual upbeat self on the voice message. Malorie wondered if she had finally come to grips with the reality that Lani was likely in grave danger. Given the time that had passed and Lani's possible connection to the death of Tina Lang, she doubted Lani's parents still believed Lani was missing of her own accord.

Malorie took a sip of her latte as she searched for Lani's name in that day's news headlines. Seeing nothing new about Lani or Tina, she went to close out of the search. She paused when another headline from that morning caught her eye.

TRIAL DATE SET FOR MURDER OF CHRIS RICHARDS, BROTHER OF SEAHAWK AND SEATTLE HOMICIDE DETECTIVE

His last name sounded familiar, and Malorie clicked on the article. As she read, she realized where she'd heard the name before. His sister was Detective Tess Richards of the Seattle Homicide Unit, the detective who had first taken Lani's case. She wondered why the detective was working missing persons instead of homicide. *Maybe it had to do with her brother's death.*

She read on, remembering when the twenty-three-year-old's brutal murder was initially in the news just after the Fourth of July. His throat had been slit at the home of a famous actor who'd retired in Seattle. He worked as a landscaper on their property, and his body was discovered in the driveway of the gated waterfront mansion.

His alleged killer, who was now wheelchair-bound from injuries sustained the night of Chris's death, had entered a plea of not guilty by reason of insanity. When Malorie got to the end of the article, there was a video clip from last Sunday's Seahawk game. She pressed play.

Chris's older brother, Nathan Richards, was a defensive lineman for the team. CenturyLink Field was filled to capacity. The video panned across Nathan standing with the team and the crowd of 72,000 people as they held a moment of silence for Chris Richards in the stadium, usually known for its record-breaking crowd noise. It was a moving scene.

"Thanks for meeting me."

VIABLE HOSTAGE

Malorie looked up at the sound of Tatiana's voice. She hardly recognized Lani's mother. She wore mismatching sweats and her dark hair looked like it hadn't been brushed in days. She wore no makeup. From the redness around her eyes, it looked like she'd recently been crying.

"Of course." Malorie set her phone on the table and started to stand from her seat.

"Don't get up, sweetheart," Tatiana said, taking a seat in the chair across from her. She hadn't bothered to get anything to drink. "I'm sorry I'm late."

"That's okay." Malorie's heart broke for what Lani's mother must be feeling.

"I thought I'd be coming from the hospital, but I called in sick last minute. I was up all night worrying about Lani, and I just couldn't bring myself to face anyone this morning." Tatiana met Malorie's gaze for the first time. "Did you know about her pregnancy?"

Malorie shook her head. "No. I just found out after the detective asked me about it. At first, I told him she couldn't be pregnant. That there was no way I wouldn't have known. But, after he left, I went into her room and found this...."

She reached into her purse and slid the ultrasound photo across the small round table. Lani's mother covered her mouth with her hand. Fresh tears fell down her cheeks as she lifted the image of her unborn grandchild.

It took her a few minutes before she was able to speak. She wiped her tears away with the back of her hand.

"I can't believe we didn't act sooner. File a report when she didn't show up for my event. Thank goodness you did." Her voice was soft, on the verge of breaking. "I just pray that it's not too late."

Malorie wished there was something she could say to

console her. But what would she say? She didn't want to do Lani's mom the disservice of pretending everything might be okay. "Me too."

"I feel that I failed her as a mother. I was always so focused on my work. It always came before the family. I even pushed my children to become doctors, even though I know Lani never loved medicine like I do. I didn't mean to, but—" She cleared her throat. "I know I made Lani feel that to do anything else would be a disappointment to me. And, I'm afraid, now I'll never have the chance to tell her how much she means to me."

Tatiana set the ultrasound photo back onto the table before using her finger to dab the tears from the corners of her eyes. "Can I keep this?"

"Yes. That's why I brought it."

She nodded. "Thank you."

They sat in silence for a moment before Lani's mom pushed back her chair. "Well, I won't keep you. Thank you for meeting me. And for the photo."

"You're welcome." Malorie took a last drink from her latte before she got to her feet. Tatiana hugged her goodbye, and Malorie followed her out of the busy cafe. Malorie's phone rang as she walked toward the bus stop. She'd opted for public transportation instead of paying for downtown parking.

She pulled her phone out of her bag and it was her Uncle Wade.

"Hi," she said.

"Hey, Mal. I've got a few questions for you about some emails Lani received. Could I come by the university?"

"Actually, I'm downtown. Not that far from police headquarters. I could probably be there in ten minutes if you want to talk now."

"Great. See you in ten. I'll meet you downstairs."

CHAPTER TWENTY-FIVE

Malorie sat across from her uncle Wade in his office at Seattle Homicide. She'd never been to his work before. He'd met her at the ground-floor entrance of Police Headquarters and escorted her up to the seventh floor. She'd followed him through the large room of detectives working at their desks, the different squads separated by wooden cubicles.

Her eyes were drawn to a photo on the wall of Cody, Wade's old partner and best friend. Malorie had been in high school when Cody was killed during a high-profile arrest alongside Wade. She knew from things her mother had said that Cody's death had devastated her uncle. His alcoholism grew even worse after Cody died. Over the next several years, her mother worried it might be his demise.

Meeting her uncle at the Seattle Homicide Unit to talk about Lani was a stark reminder of the dark reality that she might never see her roommate again. She'd blinked back tears at the sight of the 1970s Ted Bundy poster on the wall next to Wade's office door. Her tears weren't because of the multitude of heinous crimes he'd committed, but because Lani would've loved to see that. She was always reading true crime, especially cases that had taken place in the Pacific

Northwest. Her fascination with criminology was the reason she was planning on becoming a forensic pathologist. Now, Malorie regretted never bringing her to see where her uncle worked.

Wade slid a small stack of papers across his desk. "I'd like you to take a look at these. First of all, do you recognize the email address they were sent from?"

Malorie took the printed emails and read through them carefully. She didn't recognize the email address they came from. They were sent to Lani's university email. Instead of a name, the sender was *Your Friend*. She was surprised to see that Lani had responded to them.

The emails were short. One or two sentences. They were all dated the week before she disappeared.

Your Friend: *I know your secret. You can't hide it any longer. Soon, everyone will know.*

Lani: *Who is this?*

Your Friend: *Meet me outside Harry's. Saturday at 8pm. Come alone.*

Malorie let the pages fall to her lap. "I have no idea who this is. It doesn't make any sense. It sounds like they were threatening to expose her pregnancy. But no one knew. *I* didn't even know."

Her uncle's face was unreadable. "I know it's upsetting she didn't tell you about it. But can you think of anyone you know who might've sent these emails?"

Malorie thought hard. "No...."

She laid the emails back on Wade's desk.

"But I obviously didn't know her as well as I thought I did."

"We've traced the IP address associated with the email to a shared computer at Elliot Bay University Medical

Center. It's password protected and only accessed by the medical center's staff. So, it could be another med student, a faculty member with privileges at the hospital, or someone she met during a clinical rotation. We really don't know."

"It could be Dr. Delaney. He works there." She stood from her seat and pointed at the stack of emails. "This could be proof it was him."

"He was three hours away when Lani left Harry's bar on Saturday night," her uncle reminded her. "He was also working at EBU Medical Center the night Tina Lang went missing."

He looked like there was more he wanted to say, but he didn't.

"Have you found out who killed Tina?"

Wade shook his head. "No."

Malorie stared at her uncle, waiting for him to give her more information. He stood from his chair and came around his desk. He placed a hand on her shoulder.

"We're working on it. Just like we're working on finding Lani. Come on, I'll walk you to your car."

They rode the elevator to the parking garage in silence. She stopped and turned to her uncle when they reached her Mazda.

"Thanks for coming," he said, giving her a fatherly hug.

"Do you think she's dead, Uncle Wade?"

Wade stepped back and looked her in the eyes. "Honestly, I don't know. If Lani's disappearance is related to Tina's death, then I think the chances are high that she might already be dead. But, we don't know for sure that they *are* related. So, until we do, I think you try to stay positive that she might still be alive and think of anything and everything you can that might help us find her. Okay?"

"I can't sleep knowing she might be out there, still alive and caged up somewhere. Or, even worse, that she's dead. I feel like I'm doing nothing to help her."

"We are all doing what we can. But I know this is hard."

Malorie nodded.

"And you feel free to call me, day or night, if you think of anything."

"Okay." Malorie reached for the driver's door and remembered that Elle was about to have her baby any day. She turned toward her uncle. "How's Elle?"

"She's good. She's been busy getting everything ready before our son comes."

"I can't wait to meet him."

Her uncle smiled. "Me too. I'll talk to you soon."

Malorie climbed into her car as her uncle walked back to the elevator. She was thankful for his involvement in Lani's case. In her late teenage years, Malorie had heard her mother say more than once that Wade was going to ruin his career by his drinking. But, contrary to her mother's fears, Wade had worked hard for the last few years to turn his life around, even though things hadn't always been easy for him. And she knew he would do whatever it took to help his detectives find Lani.

CHAPTER TWENTY-SIX

Lani had been waiting all day for her captor to return. She'd hardly slept since he'd come the day before, forcing her to walk on the treadmill again. She had planned to attempt an escape, but he kept his gun closely aimed at her head the entire time. She knew if she'd tried to break free, she would've never made it out alive. But she hated herself for not trying. For chickening out.

She'd heard voices the day before. They sounded as if they were right outside the walls she was held captive within. If she was on a houseboat, there could be neighboring boats all around her. She wouldn't have far to escape.

Her mind was reeling with what he wanted with her. And her baby. She could only hope his disguise meant he might allow her to live. Why else would he be worried about her seeing his face? But she couldn't leave her and her baby's lives to fate.

The light coming through the small window above her bed was beginning to fade. *Maybe he wasn't coming.* But he had to. She couldn't bear the thought of spending another night in that hospital bed with that sick creep watching her through the camera. And, if he'd made her walk on the treadmill yesterday, why not today?

She tried to distract herself from imagining why he was keeping her there. She needed to focus on her plan to escape. But, with nothing else to do, it wasn't easy.

She closed her eyes, even though she knew there was no way she could sleep. Although, if her captor wasn't returning until tomorrow, the best thing she could do was try to get some rest. When her chance for escape came, she needed to be strong.

She had no sooner shut her eyelids when she heard the door to her room swing open. She sat up and turned in the direction of the sound.

There he was. The same surgical mask and glasses covered his face. Same scrubs. Same lab coat. Same gun.

He held the gun down at his side as he crossed the room. Her breathing quickened when she noticed he left the key to the door in the lock. She watched him pull the key to her handcuffs out of his pocket before he moved her catheter bag from the bed to her IV pole. She held still as he pointed his gun at her chest, using his other hand to unlock the cuffs on her feet. He moved the barrel within an inch of her sternum as he undid the cuff on one of her hands.

He cuffed her hands together and grabbed her by the arm. She allowed him to help her stand. He kept the gun aimed at her chest as they moved slowly toward the treadmill. With his hand wrapped around her upper arm, she stepped onto the exercise machine. Lani placed one foot in front of the other as the belt beneath her started to move.

She glanced at her catheter bag out of the corner of her eye. She was confident she could swiftly rip out her IV, but the catheter would be much harder to remove without deflating the inner balloon. She'd have to take it with her.

VIABLE HOSTAGE

She focused on the wall in front of her as the treadmill gradually picked up speed. She tried to calm her breathing and avoided looking her masked captor in the eye. She knew now it was no use trying to see who he was. In her peripheral vision, she could see his gun remained aimed at her chest. Voices came from outside her window, and her captor cocked his head toward the sound of the neighbors.

She wrapped one hand around the gun barrel and the other around his wrist. As he turned toward her, she slammed the weapon against the treadmill. The pistol slipped from his grip and skidded across the linoleum floor. It slid under the hospital bed before coming to a stop.

Lani jumped off the treadmill, tearing her IV from her arm as she went. She grabbed her catheter bag from the IV pole and ran for the open door. His hand touched her arm, but she pulled free before he could close his grip around it.

She reached the door and swung it closed behind her. She turned the key in the lock a second before he grasped the doorknob and pulled. The door shook as he violently rattled it back and forth.

Lani veered right and ran down the narrow hallway. There was an opening at the end of the hall, leading to a spiral staircase. She stopped suddenly at the top of the staircase and turned her head back toward an open doorway. She'd seen hospital-grade monitors and IV pumps in her blurred vision when she passed by. *Was there someone else locked up who needed saving?*

She looked down at the compact living space on the main floor of the houseboat, knowing how close she was to freedom. She ripped away the duct tape that covered her mouth and pulled it down below her chin, two or three loops of tape still wrapped around the back of her head.

She turned toward the open doorway and entered the small room. It was about the same size as the one she'd been kept in. There was a desk with two computer screens on one side of the wall. One of the screens showed a live video feed of her empty bed.

A twin mattress with a pillow and blanket lay on the floor next to the desk. A camera, identical to the one in her room, was mounted in the corner of the ceiling. She moved closer to the medical equipment she'd seen from the hallway.

She held her breath as she stood over a live fetus housed in a small, sealed plastic bag that lay atop a cushioned medical stand. The bag was filled with a clear liquid that was pumped and filtered in through one side of the bag and out the other. Various water-tight ports protruded from the bag.

The infant's eyes were closed and she looked to be sleeping. One of the infant's legs jerked in a swift motion before she stilled again. The baby girl had some body fat, and, while she was still tiny, looked to be a couple months more developed than Lani's baby. She had a head of short, dark hair, and Lani guessed she weighed about three pounds.

Her umbilical cord was fed through an enclosed opening in the bag, which connected her umbilical vessels to IV tubing. The infant's blood looked to be circulated through the tubing through an oxygenating system before returning to the infant. Lani looked up at the screen above the infant that monitored the infant's heart rate and blood pressure.

Lani put her hand over her own womb and took a step back. Had that monster taken her and her baby for some sort of science experiment? *Whose baby was this? And where was her mother?*

She needed to get out. *Now.* She couldn't take the infant

with her. But she would get help, and they would come back for her.

Lani turned for the door but stopped dead in her tracks. The 'doctor' stood in the doorway.

CHAPTER TWENTY-SEVEN

Stephenson hit rush-hour traffic on his way back from the university. The sun had already disappeared behind the Olympic Mountains across the Sound when he walked past the floor-to-ceiling window before entering the Homicide Unit.

Adams looked up from his desk when Stephenson entered their cubicle. "How'd it go?"

Stephenson shrugged his shoulders before taking a seat at his desk. "Okay. Jerad's wife admitted to having his Mercedes over the weekend, but she claimed she was home alone Saturday night. Not exactly a solid alibi, but we don't have any evidence to disprove it.

"I interviewed Lani's ex after his last class. He seemed aloof about her disappearance. He said he was with two friends on Saturday night, but I'm still working on confirming his alibi with both of them."

"While you were gone, I looked through Gretchen Hogan's case file that Tess brought us earlier. There's remarkably little information. According to Gretchen's coworker, her pregnancy was a result of a one-night stand, and the father had no intention of being involved in her child's life. It's sad, really. No one, other than her coworker, seemed to express much interest in her disappearance," Adams said.

"Maybe we should speak to that coworker. See if we can learn anything that might help us link her disappearance to Tina and Lani's."

"I already called the pharmacy at EBU Medical Center where she works. She gets off in a half hour and said she'd be happy to talk to us. I told her we'd meet her at the hospital."

"Great."

"Unless you want to go by yourself and I can hit the gym."

Stephenson looked for a sign his partner was joking but didn't see one.

"I'll go."

The two of them turned at the sound of Tess's voice. Her down jacket was zipped halfway, and her purse was slung over her shoulder. "I was just on my way out. But I can go with you."

"Sounds great," Adams said.

Stephenson looked hesitant.

"I don't mind," Tess said. "I'd like to. Technically, Gretchen Hogan is still my missing persons case."

"Okay, let's go."

"See you tomorrow," Adams said.

Stephenson grabbed his coat and followed her out.

Tess was quiet for the first few minutes of the drive. She looked out the passenger side window as her boyfriend drove.

VIABLE HOSTAGE

"Think you'll be ready to come back to Homicide next month?" Stephenson asked.

She let out a deep breath. "I guess I'll have to be."

In the months since her brother's murder, she hadn't often talked about it. Even though Blake knew that Chris, and his death, was constantly on her mind.

"Did you ever go back to that therapist?" he asked.

"The grief counselor?"

"Yeah."

"No."

He could feel her eyes on him as he changed lanes. He wished there was some way to take her pain away. But all he could do was be there for her when, and if, she wanted to talk about it.

"I got my vacation approved so I can go to Chris's trial. At least for the first two weeks. I'm going to see if I can take a little more time, in case the trial goes longer."

Stephenson reached for her hand. "I'm sorry I wasn't able to get the time off to be there with you. It's this new case with Wade's niece."

"It's okay. I know you wanted to be." She enfolded her fingers into his.

"I just hope the jury doesn't buy that insanity plea. It's so ridiculous," she added after a moment.

Stephenson knew she was also worried the injuries Chris's killer sustained the night of his murder might be a cause for sympathy from the jury.

"There will be enough witness testimony that they'll see the truth."

She nodded. "Sometimes," her voice came out a whisper, "I just still can't believe he's gone."

"I know." He turned toward her after he stopped at a

red light.

A comfortable silence passed between them until they reached the hospital.

"You're going to get justice for your brother." Stephenson pulled into the hospital parking garage and parked in an open space on the second floor. "I love you," he said as he opened the driver's door.

Tess squeezed his hand before letting go. "I love you too."

"We're here to speak with Monica Fulton," Stephenson said after introducing themselves to the man behind the glass partition at the hospital pharmacy entrance.

The young man looked inquisitively at the detectives. "I'll go find her. Be right back."

Less than a minute later, a middle-aged woman wearing scrubs came through the door next to the window. Her auburn hair was pulled back into a low ponytail.

"Hi," she said, shaking hands with the detectives. "I'm Monica."

"You spoke with my partner, Detective Adams, on the phone," Stephenson said. "I'm Detective Stephenson and this is Detective Richards."

Tess glanced at the young man staring at them from behind the partition to the pharmacy. "Is there somewhere we can talk privately?"

Monica nodded. "The cafeteria is on this same floor. We can talk there."

"Great," Tess said as she and Blake followed her down the busy hospital hallway lined with framed photos of physicians who had practiced there over the years.

VIABLE HOSTAGE

There were several empty tables when they reached the cafeteria. The three of them sat at the first one they approached.

Monica looked eagerly across the table from the detectives. "Do you have any news about Gretchen? Have you found her?"

"No, I'm afraid not," Tess said.

Monica folded her hands atop the table. "I figured that was probably too good to be true."

"We're just looking for a little more information," Stephenson said.

"Okay. Although I don't think there's anything I haven't already told the missing persons detective who followed up with the report."

"Was her pregnancy common knowledge among her friends and coworkers?" Stephenson asked.

"Well, yeah, she was five months along. It would've been hard to hide at that point. And she didn't have many friends. Just me. She'd made a lot of bad choices. Pushed a lot of people away."

"But not you?" Tess asked.

Monica shrugged her shoulders. "I always had a soft spot for her I guess. She had a good heart. And, after she found out she was pregnant, she really turned things around. She wanted to be a good mother." Monica looked back and forth between the detectives. "Which is why I knew she wouldn't have disappeared like that on purpose." Her gaze fell to her hands. "I should've filed the report sooner. She hadn't answered my calls for a few days. I should've gone to her apartment to check on her, but I didn't. We work twelve-hour shifts, and when I went back to work after having four days off, I learned Gretchen hadn't shown up for her last two shifts. That night, I went to her apartment. Her car was there, but she didn't answer her door. I had a spare key, so I let myself in. She wasn't there. That's when I filed the report." She blinked away the tears that brimmed her eyes. "But, it was obviously too late."

Neither of the detectives refuted her statement.

"According to the report, you didn't know who the father of her child was. You said he wasn't involved in Gretchen's life," Stephenson said. "You still don't have any idea who it might've been?"

Monica shook her head. "Honestly, I don't think Gretchen even knew who it was. Her pregnancy was a result of a one-night stand, and that's all she ever told me. Why are you asking all these questions now?"

Tess and Blake exchanged a look.

"We're exploring the possibility that her disappearance might be connected to a couple of other women who've gone missing in the last few months," Stephenson said.

Monica bit her lip. "Like the one found on the shore of Alki Beach?"

Tess glanced at her boyfriend. His eyes didn't waver from Gretchen's.

"Yes," he said.

Monica's eyes grew wide.

"We don't know for sure if they're connected," Stephenson added. "But we're looking into the possibility."

"Oh my...."

"Thank you for meeting with us. We really appreciate your help."

"Um. Of course." Monica looked to be in a daze as they stood from the table.

"Please let us know if you think of anything else that

could help us."

"I will."

Tess gave her a warm smile before she and Stephenson headed back to their car.

"Well, that didn't seem very helpful," Tess said when they reached the parking garage.

"Actually, I think it was. What she told us makes me more convinced Gretchen's disappearance is connected to Tina and Lani."

"Because she was pregnant?"

"And, because other than Monica, no one seemed to care that she was gone."

Tess opened the driver's door of his unmarked Ford.

"Have you had dinner?" Blake asked.

"No, but I'm not really hungry."

"Well, I'm starving. Why don't we grab a burger or something on our way back? Maybe there's some more you can tell me about Tina and Lani's missing persons cases. Plus, I've hardly seen you outside of work in weeks."

Tess eyed him playfully before getting into the car. "Are you wanting to spend more time with me or are you just using me to help with your case?"

He smiled. "Both."

CHAPTER TWENTY-EIGHT

Jerad Delaney found his wife sitting alone in the formal dining room of their Lake Washington waterfront estate when he got home from his bail hearing. A half-full glass of whiskey sat on the mahogany table in front of her.

"I saw on the news they released you. I thought you would've been home a couple hours ago," Carolyn said before taking a drink.

Jerad stood at the opposite end of the table from his wife. "It took us awhile to get away from the courthouse because of all the press. We hit traffic on the way home."

"I'm sure I don't have to tell you how humiliating this is for me."

But not surprising, since she was already aware of his crimes. They'd never spoken about the videos she'd sent him as blackmail. If she turned them over, he would undoubtedly be convicted.

"Just when the world seemed to be forgetting what you were accused of years ago. A scandal like this could end my career at the university."

If she really was upset about his arrest, he wondered why she'd been threatening to release the videos to the police for the last few months. *Had she been bluffing?*

"A homicide detective came to the university today and questioned me about your students, Tina Lang and Lani Wu. He seemed to think I might have something to do with Tina's murder and Lani's disappearance. Did you give them that idea?" she asked.

"No," he said. "I did not."

He studied his wife of twenty years from across the room. The most cold-hearted human being he had ever known. Her revenge killings of his two students were the only thing she'd ever done that showed him she cared. Only, he knew now that she hadn't done it out of jealousy. She'd done it to get back at him for ruining her career.

She'd had ambitions to be much more than the president of EBU. She'd planned to run for Washington State governor years back, with dreams of one day running for President. But, when Jerad was accused of rape eight years ago, her political campaign was halted before it even began. And she hated him for it.

He had thought they were in love when they were married. But he soon learned it was a marriage of convenience. She hoped being married to a doctor would help elevate her status in the academic community.

She'd never loved him. He'd been a pawn.

He could've divorced her, but, for the first half of their marriage, he'd held out hope she would love him back. When he couldn't get what he wanted, he turned his obsession to his students. Students that looked just like Carolyn had when he'd fallen in love with her. Now, her blackmail seemed to be the only thing holding them together.

"If you're convicted, I'll be filing for divorce." She

downed what was left in her glass before getting up from the table.

He debated whether to ask her about the video. "Is your son home?"

"I would hope after twenty years of being his stepfather, you could refer to him as *our* son."

She didn't seem to catch the irony of her remark after just threatening divorce. And, she was the reason for the lack of bond they shared. He had wanted to be a father to her son, but he'd always resented Jerad. A resentment fueled by his mother.

"No, he's not." Carolyn avoided eye contact as she brushed past him. "I'm going to bed. It's been an exhausting twenty-four hours since your arrest."

After she left the dining room, he knew he wouldn't see her until the next morning. He'd been sleeping in their guest room for years. Hearing her shut the door to the master bedroom upstairs, Jerad made his way to his office on the main floor of their home.

He shut the door behind him and pulled his silver cigar case out of his desk drawer. He opened the case, which housed three vials of propofol along with needles and syringes that he kept for rare occasions like tonight. When he needed something stronger than fentanyl or midazolam.

He removed a needle and syringe from their packaging and withdrew the contents of one of the vials. He took off his shoe and sock before plunging the contents of the syringe into a vein atop his foot. He grabbed a tissue from his desk to stop the bleeding after he extracted the needle.

As he closed the cigar case, he wasn't sure what would be worse: waking up tomorrow morning or dying in his sleep.

CHAPTER TWENTY-NINE

Elle's younger sister, Kayla, pulled her car away from the curb as Wade turned into his drive. He waved at his sister-in-law as their cars came within a few feet from each other. But Kayla refused to make eye contact. She sped away without so much as a glance in his direction.

Wade knew he had never done anything to make Kayla distrust him. He guessed her reservations about him were mainly because of Elle's first husband. While it was annoying to receive the cold shoulder when he hadn't done anything to deserve it, he was willing to give her some time to accept him. He hoped Elle was right and she would come around to him eventually. And, that *eventually* came sooner rather than later.

"You hungry?"

Elle was unloading the dishwasher when Wade entered their kitchen. It was the first night that week he'd gotten home before she went to bed. Her dark hair was pulled into a high ponytail, and Wade admired how beautiful she was, nine months pregnant with his child.

"Not really," he said.

"Kayla came over for dinner so there's some leftover pad thai in the fridge if you want some."

Wade set his laptop bag on the kitchen counter before embracing his wife in a hug. She refrained from asking about Lani, knowing if he had some good news, he would've told her.

"Thank you," he said. "How was Kayla?"

"Fine."

He knew by the look on Elle's face she was holding something back from him. He waited for her to elaborate.

"She doesn't think you'll make it to the birth."

"What? Of course I will. I've made arrangements with the department to take time off. I'm not a detective anymore. It's not like I'm in the middle of a case." Except that he was doing everything he could to help find Lani. He'd even stuck his neck out to expedite her case being transferred to Homicide from Missing Persons.

Now, it was Elle's turn to give him a knowing look.

"That's ridiculous. I'll be there." Wade opened the fridge, wishing for a cold beer even though they didn't keep alcohol in the house. He pushed the thought from his mind as he closed the door and opted for a glass of water. "Then, she'll see what a perfect and loving husband I am. *And*, the brother-in-law she's always wanted."

Across the kitchen, Elle bit her lip before giving in to a chuckle. "If you say so."

CHAPTER THIRTY

Lani placed her other hand over her uterus.

Her captor held his gun at his side and lifted the small key to her room in his other hand. *Had she not locked the door completely in her panic to get away from him? Or did he just break through in rage?* She watched him slip the key into the pocket of his lab coat before he held out his hand toward her.

Lani looked around the small room for another option, but there was nowhere to go.

"Please," she said. "Don't do this."

She stood still, refusing to go to him. He stepped into the room. Lani stiffened. He continued to move toward her. Blood dripped down her arm from where she'd pulled out her IV.

He grabbed her forearm. She tried to pull away, but her movements were limited by the handcuffs.

Lani sank to her knees and began to sob as he dragged her out of the room.

"Please, just let me go," she cried.

When they reached the corridor, he forcefully pulled her to her feet. She dug her heels into the floor as he pulled her in the direction of her room. He stopped and pressed the barrel of his pistol against her temple as if to let her know what would happen to her if she kept fighting him.

Her breathing quickened, and she allowed him to lead her back after he pulled the gun away from her face. It was better than getting shot in the head. She slowed when they reached the doorway to her room. He shoved her inside.

She let him cuff her wrists and ankles to the rails of the bed. He withdrew a roll of duct tape from his scrub pocket and wrapped a long strip around her head a few times. After adhering the tape to the skin around her lips, he pulled a needle and syringe from his pocket.

She recoiled against the bed. She should've screamed when she had the chance. She'd been so shocked by finding the fetus in the other room that she missed her opportunity to call for help.

She jerked her arm to the side as the needle made contact with her skin. He turned toward her, and she could see her weathered reflection in his mirrored protective eyewear. Lani grimaced as he injected the cold solution into one of her antecubital veins in the crook of her arm.

Without a word, he left her alone in her cell. After a few minutes, she felt her body relax from the injection he'd given her and from knowing he was gone. At least for now. Lani noticed he'd left the door to her room open. She wondered if that meant he was coming back.

She awoke from a light sleep a few minutes later when the light came on in her room. She watched her captor unroll a large tarp on the floor before bringing a tray of medical equipment into the small space. He left the tray next to the bed and went to retrieve another tray, this one bigger than the last. Lani sat forward in her bed when she saw the empty plastic bag that lay atop the cushioned tray, just like the one the fetus had been lying in.

Lani's eyes widened as she watched her masked captor unfold the tarp. He worked for the next few minutes to slide it between Lani and her mattress. Lani kicked and flailed beneath her containment. After the tarp was in place, he shoved her against the mattress. Lani squirmed beneath his hold as best she could in her drugged state. Despite her movements, he strapped her upper body to the bed, followed by her legs.

She again caught a terrifying reflection of herself in the mirrored plastic that covered his eyes. Lani struggled to lift herself away from the mattress. But the straps were too tight.

She felt a prick on the inside of her arm as he injected her with another solution. She became aware of the effect the drug was having on her central nervous system. Her breathing began to slow as she watched the mystery doctor put on a pair of sterile gloves.

She wished now that she would've fought harder. Maybe a bullet to the head would've been better than what was about to happen. Her breath caught in her chest as he lifted a scalpel from the stand beside her bed.

"Try to hold still. This is gonna hurt," he said, revealing his voice for the first time.

Lani screamed through the duct tape as the blade cut through her abdominal wall.

CHAPTER THIRTY-ONE

Wade closed his laptop and stood from his chair. He hadn't meant to work so late. Again. It just didn't feel right going home after only an eight-hour day when Malorie's best friend was still missing. Not when there were things he could do to help.

He was surprised to see his lieutenant, Will Greyson, appear in his doorway when he reached for his coat.

"Can I see you in my office for a minute?"

It was rare to see the lieutenant in the building past five o'clock.

"Sure," Wade said.

He followed his much-shorter superior through the homicide unit. They had worked together for nearly twenty years, and Wade had never liked him. The only thing the two men had in common was a tendency to live for the job. But for entirely different reasons.

Greyson reveled in the authority the job gave him. It had always struck Wade as compensation for some inadequacy Greyson must have perceived in himself. Now, as a lieutenant, he loved to use his rank as an excuse to tell others what to do. And the kudos and prestige he received from the position.

Wade, on the other hand, simply gave a damn about the victims. Something inside him longed for justice for those who'd had their lives taken from them. Before he became a sergeant, Wade could never let go of any of his cases until their killer was caught. There were a few unsolved that still gnawed at him.

The Seattle Slasher's killings got to him more than any other. But, fortunately, those cases were now solved.

Wade's late father was still a detective with Seattle Homicide when Greyson started as a rookie detective. Wade smiled at the thought that his dad hadn't liked him any more than Wade did.

When they got to his office, Wade could see through the glass wall that he wasn't the only one who'd been summoned. Stephenson was already seated across from the lieutenant's large desk.

Wade stepped through the doorway. Unlike his own office, the lieutenant's offered a view of the Seattle waterfront. A lit-up Bainbridge ferry was making its way across the Sound.

Greyson closed the door behind him and Wade braced himself for whatever unpleasantries lay ahead. Greyson moved behind his desk and sat in his leather chair. He motioned for Wade to sit beside Stephenson.

The lieutenant cleared his throat and turned to Stephenson. Wade noticed Greyson had buzzed what remained of his graying hair.

"As you may not be aware, our Chief of Police and Carolyn Delaney, the EBU President, go back a long way. They attended Ballard High together. Which is why the

VIABLE HOSTAGE

Chief was especially unhappy to get a complaint from his old friend about being questioned regarding your recent homicide case at the university."

So that's what this is about, Wade thought. He should've known it would be something ridiculous. Like being affluent and powerful gave her cause to be above the law. But the lieutenant could never resist an opportunity to throw his weight around.

"Just doing my job, Lieutenant," Stephenson said.

"That's what I told the Chief. And I'm sure you were."

Yeah right, Wade thought.

"Just make sure you have the evidence to substantiate any further involvement of the EBU president in your investigation so I don't have to hear about it again from the Chief of Police."

That was more like it. Wade knew Greyson loved the excuse to play boss.

"Yes, sir," Stephenson said.

Wade could tell the young detective was holding back what he would really like to say.

"All right. I won't keep you any longer."

Stephenson and Wade stood from their chairs.

"Hold on, Sergeant," Wade heard Greyson say before he followed Stephenson out.

He turned back to face the lieutenant. *What now?*

"I was hoping I wouldn't have to say this, but I want to remind you that just because your niece's roommate is missing, it doesn't give you a right to be involved in her case. In fact, it should be the opposite. It's a conflict of interest. You shouldn't have *any* involvement in these cases.

"I know you've been working even later than usual this week, and I saw your niece here with you yesterday. I heard you were questioning her about some emails that had been sent to her roommate."

"Yeah."

"If your niece needs to be questioned again about her roommate, you make sure it's done by someone who's not related to her. And leave her roommate's case to be investigated by the detectives who are actually assigned to it."

Wade's phone chimed and he pulled his cell out of his pocket. Greyson made no effort to hide his annoyance as Wade checked his phone screen. Seeing the text, Wade turned for the door.

"I have to go. My wife's in labor."

CHAPTER THIRTY-TWO

Malorie still didn't know if she passed her anesthesia and radiology midterms, but, after taking yesterday's midterm, she had felt that it had gone much better. She could only pray that she'd passed the other two.

She'd spent the day in a clinical rotation in the OR at EBU Medical Center, which had turned out to be mundane. She'd hoped to at least see one cardiac procedure since the medical center was ranked in the top ten cardiology and heart surgery hospitals in the US. However, there hadn't been any scheduled for today. Instead she observed a total knee replacement, an appendectomy, and a rotator cuff repair. While they were interesting, they weren't what she was passionate about.

Her grandfather had passed away from a heart attack only two years after he retired as a Seattle homicide detective. It was just days before Malorie's thirteenth birthday. She would never forget the way her mother sank to the kitchen floor when she got the call. He was a great man and had become the first African American homicide detective for the Seattle Police Department. Her uncle Wade had followed in his father's footsteps. Her grandfather's death played a large part in what had made her want to become a cardiologist. If he'd had more preventative care, he might still be alive.

Malorie drummed her highlighter against her textbook as she sat on the couch in her apartment. She stared out the window at the lights from the rush-hour traffic crossing the bridge over the Fremont Cut, the canal that connected Lake Washington and Lake Union to Puget Sound. She hadn't been able to concentrate on her studies all week. But this was the first time she wasn't thinking of Lani.

She couldn't stop thinking about how Luke looked when he'd sat next to her during their midterm the day before. Even his hands were hot. While they were taking the exam, her eyes had wandered to his long, lean fingers. She'd noticed his hands were still tan from the summer. She wondered how it would feel to have them touch her. All over.

Her phone's ringtone interrupted her daydream. She didn't recognize the number.

"Hello?"

"Hi, is this Malorie?"

"Yes."

"This is Dr. Campbell."

Malorie wondered why her cardiology professor would be calling her at this time in the evening. "Oh. Hi."

"I just got a call from a colleague of mine at Elliot Bay University Medical Center. He's going to be assisting in an emergency coronary artery bypass graft tonight and wanted to know if I had a student who would like to observe. I know you've been wanting to see one, so I thought I'd see if you'd like to scrub in tonight and watch the procedure?"

VIABLE HOSTAGE

Malorie stood from her couch. "Yes. Thank you. I would."

"Great. How soon can you be there?"

"Probably twenty minutes."

"Okay. Natalie is the charge nurse in the OR tonight. I'll let her know you're coming."

"All right. Thank you."

"You're welcome. See you Monday."

Her apartment was less than two miles from the hospital, and Malorie drove as fast as she could without risking getting a ticket. She couldn't believe she was going to see a CABG procedure tonight. She'd only seen them done on TV and in videos in class.

She was always amazed when the anesthesiologist would inject potassium into the patient's IV bag to stop the heart long enough for the surgeons to work on the organ without it beating in their hands. And how the patient's body was cooled at the beginning of the procedure to slow their metabolism. That way, they could extend the amount of time the patient's circulation could be sustained by a heart and lung machine known to medical professionals as ECMO, or extracorporeal membrane oxygenation.

After arriving at the hospital, Malorie parked her car in the overflow parking area that was free for med students. She hurried to the main entrance. When she reached the elevator, she pushed the button for the third floor. She leaned against the side of the elevator as the doors closed. The best thing about watching the surgery tonight was it would help distract her from imagining what had happened to Lani…and from daydreaming about Luke. At least for a little while.

Natalie was waiting for her at the OR nurse's desk like Dr. Campbell had said. She used her ID to let Malorie into the women's locker room to change. Malorie stuffed her clothes into a small locker and changed into the hospital scrubs as fast as she could. The surgery had already started, and she didn't want to miss any more of the procedure than she already had. She pulled her phone out of her purse to silence it and saw she had a new email in her university account. She could see from the notification that lit up her phone that the email was from *Your Friend*.

Her heart skipped a beat as she opened her inbox. Just like the ones to Lani, it was short. Only two sentences. *Malorie, I see you. Stop before you get hurt.*

She forwarded the message to Wade before calling his cell. It went to voicemail and she left a message. "Wade, it's Malorie. Check your email. I just forwarded you a message I got from the same person who was emailing Lani."

She hung up and checked the time on the email. It was sent only five minutes ago. From what Wade had said, the email had only been accessed from a shared hospital computer. But Dr. Delaney had been placed on leave. It would seem pretty conspicuous for him to be walking the halls of the hospital after his front-page news story. She hoped he had sent it from his home and that Wade would be able to trace it.

She couldn't take her phone into the OR. She figured there was nothing more for her to do now. She'd sent her uncle the email. Plus, she'd be safe in the OR watching the open heart, even if Dr. Delaney was on the premises. She put her phone in her purse and stuffed it on top of her clothes before closing her locker door.

VIABLE HOSTAGE

She stopped at the double doors that led to the operating rooms and put on a hat, mask, and booties from the boxes that hung on the wall. Natalie had told her to go to OR Eight after she scrubbed. Malorie pressed the button on the wall to open the automatic doors.

She moved swiftly down the quiet hallway and stopped at the large stainless steel sink outside OR Eight. After removing a scrub brush from its packaging, she leaned over the sink and wet her arms up to her elbows. She wasn't sure if she needed to scrub in since she was only observing, but there was no one to ask. She vigorously scrubbed for the next few minutes, and her fear over the threatening email was gradually replaced by excitement for what she was about to observe.

Malorie took a deep breath before entering the OR. Two surgeons and a scrub technician stood over the patient's chest with their heads down. A circulating nurse and anesthesiologist turned in Malorie's direction when she came through the door. The nurse approached Malorie, her eyes scanning Malorie's ID badge before she spoke.

"You must be our med student," the tall woman said.

Malorie nodded. "Yes."

"Come stand over here." She pointed to a space near the patient's head. "You'll be able to get a better view of what's happening. They're just about to stop the heart."

Malorie moved closer to the patient but was unable to see beyond the surgeon who was bent over the patient's chest.

"Here."

Malorie turned at the nurse's voice. She placed a stool on the floor next to her. "You can stand on this."

"Thank you," Malorie said as she stepped onto the metal stand.

Now she had a clear view of the patient's exposed chest cavity. It was incredible. The patient's rib cage was held open by a metal retractor as the surgeons worked. Behind the surgeon on the other side of the patient's body, a nurse monitored the heart and lung machine that would take over the patient's circulation when they stopped the heart.

Another surgeon stood beside a sterile tray next to the patient's leg. Malorie saw she had already removed a large part of the saphenous vein, which lay on a sterile cloth atop the tray. The saphenous vein was the longest vein in the body, and was what the surgeons would use to bypass the patient's blocked coronary arteries.

Malorie returned her focus to the patient's exposed heart. The two surgeons worked intently as they prepared to graft the saphenous vein onto the coronary vessels. It didn't seem they had even noticed she was there.

"I thought I saw Delaney here earlier."

Malorie felt a sudden chill from the surgeon's comment.

"Really?" the other surgeon asked, as he reached for a pair of forceps from the scrub technician. "I thought he was placed on leave after his arrest two days ago."

"Yeah, but I'm pretty sure it was him."

Malorie felt the small hairs stand up on the back of her neck.

"Do you think he's guilty?" the scrub technician asked.

"Well, it's not the first time he's been accused of something like this," one of the surgeons said.

"I've caught him checking me out a few times," the female surgeon chimed in as she worked to close the incision on the patient's leg. "I've heard stories from some of the nurses too. He's a perv."

"The potassium is in," the anesthesiologist announced.

"Okay. Clamp please," the surgeon held his hand out to the scrub technician.

Malorie watched the patient's heart stop beating, but she struggled to focus on the intricate work of the surgeons as they prepped the right coronary artery for the bypass. She tried to shake Dr. Delaney from her thoughts and concentrate on the amazing procedure in front of her. She'd been waiting a long time to see this.

"We're ready for the saphenous."

The female surgeon carefully lifted the vein from the sterile tray.

"Did you say you thought you saw Dr. Delaney tonight?" the anesthesiologist asked. "I saw him earlier too. He was leaving the surgical unit upstairs. I was surprised he'd still be working after his arrest."

He's here, Malorie thought. *He's who sent me that email. Which would also mean, he's the one who sent them to Lani.* She needed to tell her uncle. And get away from the hospital. Away from Dr. Delaney.

She jumped off the stool and rushed toward the doors, bumping into an empty Mayo stand.

"Are you okay?" she heard the circulating nurse ask.

She turned before leaving. "Um. No, sorry," was all she could manage.

She raced down the empty hall and pressed the button for the automatic doors leading to the nurse's station. The doors opened, and Malorie watched a tall man walk past the other side of the nurse's station.

Like Malorie, he also wore a surgical mask and hat. All she could see was his eyes and the base of his hair. But she knew immediately who he was. He strode past the desk, which was now unattended, without a glance in her direction.

He used his ID to unlock the door to a supply room at the end of the hall and went inside. Malorie heard the door lock when it closed behind him. She followed after him, slowing when she reached the supply room. She peered through the small window in the door.

Dr. Delaney's back was to her. He faced the medication dispensing system that could be found on every unit in the hospital. Because the OR was the only place in the medical center where patients underwent general anesthesia, their dispensing system contained certain drugs that weren't regularly stocked on the other floors.

Dr. Delaney was logged into the system, and Malorie watched him pull four vials from the dispenser and slide them into the side pocket of his scrubs. *Were they for his next victim? For her?*

Malorie was still gaping through the window when he turned. Dr. Delaney caught her eyes before she could move. He recognized her. She knew it. She turned. There was still no one to be found at the nurse's desk. She heard the door of the supply room open and she ran for the women's locker room.

CHAPTER THIRTY-THREE

Jerad knew it was a risk coming to the hospital when he'd been suspended due to his criminal charges. But he needed the drugs. Who knew when he'd have access to them again? He'd waited until after hours, when the only surgeries being performed, if any, would be emergencies. He worried the hospital might've already revoked his access to the drug dispensing system, but, fortunately, he'd still been able to log on.

Carolyn had already left for the university when he'd woken that morning, groggy from the amount of propofol he'd injected himself with the night before. He knew he didn't deserve it, but God had given him another day.

He withdrew as many midazolam, fentanyl, and propofol vials as he could fit in the pockets of his scrubs. He logged out of the system and turned to leave when he saw the face of his nosy student, Malorie, peering at him through the window of the door to the medication room. She was the same student he'd caught staring at the blood Carolyn had left on his Mercedes.

His eyes narrowed. Malorie spun around and turned away from the door. She'd recognized him. He was sure of it. But what could he do? The hospital would have a record of him withdrawing the drugs that filled his pockets, but he didn't care. *What good was a medical license in prison anyway?*

When he got back to the men's locker room to collect his clothes, he saw that he'd gotten a text message from the number Carolyn had been using to send him blackmail messages. *I know you're here. Meet me in the OR waiting area. Bring your keys. I need your car.*

Jerad left his belongings in his open locker and stormed out of the locker room. This had to end. Enough was enough. He marched through the empty halls to the OR's after hours waiting room. It would mean Carolyn would turn over her videos to the police, and he'd be going to prison for rape. *So be it.* He wasn't going down for two counts of murder. Or more. If she wanted his car, Carolyn's killing spree must not be over.

He pushed open the door to the waiting room, surprised to see that the person standing alone in the waiting area was not his wife.

CHAPTER THIRTY-FOUR

Adams stretched his arms above his head and turned to his partner, whose eyes were glued to his computer screen. "I think I'm going to call it a day. We've been here twelve hours, and I feel like we're no closer to solving Tina's murder and Lani's disappearance than we were this morning. I'm gonna hit the gym."

Stephenson rapidly typed something into his keyboard. "Wait. Check this out."

Adams got up from his chair and leaned over his partner's shoulder.

"Looks like a houseboat," Adams said.

"Yeah. After I spoke with Carolyn yesterday, I couldn't stop thinking about their Mercedes. The one Malorie swears had blood on the bumper Monday morning. She might've not seen the license plate, but Malorie's convinced that's the car she saw on Saturday night. I don't think we can ignore that."

"So, why are we looking at a satellite photo of a houseboat on Lake Union?" Adams asked.

"There's something that bothers me about Jerad and Carolyn. I feel like they both know more than they're telling us. I've been looking into them all day, and I found they have an adult son. His listed address matches theirs. And, he's a med student at EBU. In the same cohort as Lani. He also works as a pharmacy technician at EBU Medical Center. The same place as Gretchen Hogan, the pregnant woman who went missing at the end of May. I called the pharmacy and they confirmed he wasn't working last Saturday...or August fifteenth, the night Tina Lang was last seen. They said he only works occasionally during the school year."

"I still don't understand why we're looking at a houseboat."

"Although his listed address is the same as his parents', he's been leasing this houseboat since last May." Stephenson turned around to face Adams. "I think he's the one who sent Lani those emails and picked her up in front of Harry's on Saturday night in Jerad Delaney's Mercedes. This houseboat could be where he's keeping Lani and where he kept Tina before he killed her."

Adams folded his arms and looked pensively at the image on Stephenson's laptop. "That's a pretty big yacht parked right next to it."

"Jerad Delaney has a yacht registered in his name," Stephenson continued. "I think this is it. I checked out some older satellite footage, and it looks like the yacht was kept at the Delaney's dock on Lake Washington until their son started renting the houseboat in May. According to the marina, this houseboat is on their largest moorage space."

"How does a med student afford that?"

"Probably with a little help from mom and dad. The yacht could be what their son used to dump Tina's body into the Sound."

VIABLE HOSTAGE

"Hey guys."

They turned to see Tess standing in the middle of their cubicle. There was a look of urgency on her face.

"I just got a call from a detective on Bainbridge Island. They got the DNA result back on the skeletal hand that was found by a crabber in July. It was Gretchen Hogan's."

Stephenson and Adams exchanged a look.

"Looks like you may have found our man," Adams said to his partner.

"Who?" Tess asked.

Stephenson stood from his chair.

"I'm going to go to Jerad and Carolyn's house and see if I can get their son to come back here for an interview. If he's not there, I'll find out where he is. I don't want to tip him off by showing up at the houseboat before we have a warrant." He squeezed Tess's hand as he passed by her. "Thank you."

"I'll do the paperwork to request a search warrant for that houseboat while you're gone," Adams said as he sat down at his desk. "So much for the gym."

CHAPTER THIRTY-FIVE

Natalie was coming out of the locker room when Malorie got there. She breathed a sigh of relief as it dawned on her that she couldn't have gotten in the locked room without Natalie anyway. She turned, checking if Dr. Delaney had followed her. She was surprised to see he hadn't.

"Are you okay?" Natalie asked.

"Um…no." She knew she should tell Natalie what she had seen, but she first wanted to get out of the hospital. Away from Dr. Delaney. She needed to talk to her uncle. "I'm not feeling well, actually."

"I can see that," Natalie said. "You look flushed."

"I'm sorry, but I need to go home."

"Of course." Natalie held the locker-room door open for Malorie. "Are you okay to drive yourself home?"

She looked genuinely concerned, and Malorie thought she was probably a very good nurse.

"Yeah, I'll be fine. Thank you."

"All right. Take care of yourself."

Natalie left Malorie alone to change back into her clothes. Malorie kept her eyes on the locker-room door handle for the sixty seconds it took her to throw off her scrubs and get back into her jeans and sweatshirt. She grabbed her purse and rushed out.

Fortunately, the hallway was empty. She hurried out of the OR, pulling her phone from her purse as she went. She saw her uncle hadn't returned her call or email as she rode the elevator to the ground level. She tried calling him again, but she still got his voicemail.

"Uncle Wade, it's Malorie again. I need to talk to you. Dr. Delaney was at the hospital tonight. It looked like he was stealing drugs. I'm just leaving. Please call me."

Malorie dropped her phone back into her purse as she stepped outside. She zipped up her sweatshirt as she walked the two blocks to her car. She was glad to see the streets outside the hospital were fairly well-lit. She was uneasy, however, at the lack of people outside the hospital. She'd only passed one person on the way to her car. Thankfully, it hadn't seemed that Dr. Delaney had followed her.

She relaxed once she reached her car and locked the doors after getting inside. She set her purse on the passenger seat and turned her keys in the ignition. Her engine made a sound for a split second before it cut out. Her heart sank. *Not again.* She turned her keys once more. This time there was nothing but silence.

She swore and smacked her palm against the steering wheel. She was only a few cars down from a street lamp and decided to get out and take a look. Maybe she could jiggle the wires like her uncle had shown her on the weekend.

She popped the hood and leaned over to find the wires. She reached in to adjust them when a voice directly behind her made her jump.

"Hey."

She smacked her head against the hood.

VIABLE HOSTAGE

"Sorry. Malorie, it's Luke."

She turned around, bringing her hand up to the back of her head. Seeing his gorgeous, friendly face, she let her body rest against her front bumper.

"I didn't mean to startle you," he said.

She smiled. "It's all right. I shouldn't be so jumpy."

"You having car trouble?"

"Yeah. It's happened before. I think I've blown a fuse. My uncle looked at it last weekend and told me to buy a spare, but with Lani going missing, I forgot."

"You want me to take a look? I've done some work on cars before."

"Sure." Malorie stepped aside. She watched him use his phone as a flashlight and tinker with the same wires her uncle had.

"Why don't you try and start it one more time," he said.

Malorie climbed into the driver's seat and turned the ignition again. Nothing.

Luke came around the side of her car. "I think you're right. It's the fuse. Want a ride home? I can take you to buy one tomorrow morning and bring you back here if you want."

"Are you sure?" she asked.

"I don't mind. I'm this way."

"Are you just getting done with your clinical?" she asked as they walked.

"Yeah. A trauma patient came in at the end of the shift, so I stuck around for a while."

"Where are you parked?" Malorie asked as he led her out of the overflow parking area.

"In the physician's parking by the side entrance."

Malorie turned her head to look at him. "You know med students don't count as physicians, right?"

He laughed. "I know. I've been borrowing my stepdad's car while mine's been in the shop for the last week."

"I didn't know your dad was a doctor."

"Stepdad. How about, instead of me taking you home, you come back to my houseboat with me? It's on Lake Union, and my parents' yacht is docked next to it. We could sit out on the water, share a bottle of wine, get to know each other a little better."

Malorie stopped in her tracks as the taillights of a silver Mercedes blinked in response to the key fob in Luke's hand. It wasn't just any silver Mercedes. She recognized the license plate.

"Dr. Delaney is your stepdad?" How had she not known this?

Luke continued to walk to the driver's side. "Yeah. He's not any more pleasant at home than he is in the classroom. I don't normally advertise it to people, because once they realize my mother is the president of the university, they think that's how I got into medical school. And it's not. I worked for it. But it's not a secret. I thought you knew."

He turned around after opening the driver's door. Malorie hadn't moved since she recognized the vehicle. Seeing her hesitation, his disposition changed.

His eyes narrowed. "What's wrong, Malorie?"

It all made sense now. Lani would never have left the bar with Dr. Delaney. Luke had sent her those emails threatening to expose her pregnancy. Lani had met with him to protect her secret.

Luke slammed the car door and rushed toward her.

CHAPTER THIRTY-SIX

Malorie turned and ran out of the *Physician's Only* parking area. She felt Luke tug on her purse that was slung over her shoulder. Her body jerked backward before she twisted her arm out of the strap.

Luke stumbled, and she heard her bag hit the ground. Her cell phone skidded across the pavement, coming to a stop beside her feet. She slowed and crouched low to grab it but caught him out the corner of her eye. He was too close.

She left her phone on the ground and sprinted toward the side street. She got to the edge of the parking lot and turned left onto the alley behind the hospital. She'd expected the alley to have more street lamps, but it was surprisingly dark for being adjacent to such a large medical center. There was no one in sight.

She heard his footsteps on the pavement behind her. Hunting her. She ran farther down the alleyway, pushing her legs to move as fast as they could. She neared the waterfront pathway built to provide solace to patient's families and visitors. During the day, the pathway was filled with pedestrians. But at this time of night, it was vacant.

She should've taken a right out of the parking lot. The under-lit pathway led only to the secluded public park that neighbored the hospital. The scenic concrete path would become her own deathtrap. But she had no other choice. There was no place else now to run.

He's going to kill me, Malorie thought. *I'm sorry, Lani. I failed you.*

She felt him close in on her. A sharp pain ripped through her arm as he grabbed it. He drew her close to him with tremendous strength. Malorie opened her mouth to scream but was silenced by a blow from his fist to the back of her head.

She fell to the ground. The concrete felt like it was spinning as she pressed her palms against it. She blinked, trying to bring her vision back into focus.

She needed to get up. Run away. Call for help. But her body wasn't responding.

She moaned from the sting in her shoulder as he twisted her arm behind her back. She felt the sharp jab of a needle in her forearm. She tried to pull her arm out of his grasp as he plunged a cold solution into her arm. Her pain subsided when he removed the needle and let go of her wrist. She barely felt the impact from the second blow to her head before consciousness evaded her.

CHAPTER THIRTY-SEVEN

Luke stood over Malorie, who lay silent and still on the concrete path. He recapped the needle before dropping the empty syringe and vial of propofol into his pocket. He extended the fingers of his right hand. His knuckles throbbed from slamming against the back of her skull.

What a mess. Why couldn't she just have gotten into the damn car? He looked around. Fortunately, there was no one in the area at this time of night. He still couldn't take any chances.

He stretched out his hand one more time before grabbing Malorie's limp wrists. He dragged her off the path and into the thick shrubbery that lined the walkway on one side.

"I'll be right back," he said, as though she could hear him.

He jogged down the alley that led back to the physician's parking area. Malorie's purse and phone lay on the pavement. He scooped them up and turned off her phone. After getting into the Mercedes, he tossed them onto the floor of the passenger side. He drove to the end of the alley and parked as close as he could to where he'd left Malorie.

Luke was glad to see there was still no one in sight as he

ran across the grass. Malorie hadn't moved from the bushes.

He grabbed her by the ankles and pulled her out from the shrubs. He bent over and tried to pick her up, but found it was too awkward with her unable to hold onto him. He took another quick look around before pulling her back to his car by her feet.

He debated about where to put her. He thought about the passenger seat, but what if he got pulled over? She might not pass for just sleeping. That would be too risky. She'd have to go in the trunk.

He was sweating after lifting her into the small, rear compartment. It was a good thing she was shorter than her roommate. Lani probably wouldn't have fit.

He retrieved his roll of duct tape from the glove compartment. After turning her limp body on its side, he carefully taped her wrists together behind her back. Just in case.

He was careful not to speed on his way back to the houseboat. In his interactions with Malorie over the last week, he could tell that she wasn't going to stop sticking her nose into other people's business until she found answers about her roommate. He had a lot more research to conduct and couldn't afford for someone like her to get in his way.

There were only so many pregnant women he had the opportunity to take for his research. And with Lani's wild history, she had been an ideal subject. He doubted the police would've taken her disappearance seriously if Tina's body hadn't surfaced Monday morning. That had been terrible timing. He'd dumped her body into the Sound nearly two months ago. He was starting to think her remains would never be found.

He stopped at a light and tried to look relaxed for the

traffic cam. He stifled a yawn as the light turned green. He'd only gotten two hours of sleep in the last twenty-four hours. And now he had to deal with the girl in his trunk.

Lani's baby had done exceptionally well the previous night, even though he'd taken her earlier than he had planned. He'd cozied up to Lani as soon as he'd seen her suspicious baby bump at the beginning of the semester. This was their third year of medical school together, and it wasn't lost on him that the normally well-dressed Lani was suddenly wearing baggy clothes. When he'd invited her to join him in the library to study one afternoon, his suspicions had been confirmed.

He'd pretended not to notice when Lani flipped through her textbook and revealed a black and white ultrasound photo that was tucked into the spine between a couple pages. Lani quickly turned the page and started talking about one of their classmates. Luke waited an hour for her to get up to use the bathroom. While she was gone, he opened her textbook and held up the ultrasound photo. He took a mental note of the ultrasound date and how far along she was. At that time, she'd only been sixteen weeks. He'd been counting down the days until he finally took her to the houseboat.

He smiled to himself as he pressed his foot on the gas pedal, thinking of all the meticulous planning he'd done for his research. Even becoming a pharmacy technician earlier in the year had been part of his plan to have access to the drugs he would need for his studies.

Med school wasn't even hard for him. He felt a sense of pride at what he was accomplishing while still managing passing grades.

But, there was still a lot of work to be done. And two

subjects wouldn't be enough of a research sample size. He needed more. Over the next two years, he was sure he would find some.

He pulled into the parking lot closest to his houseboat. He smiled, thinking of the look on his stepfather's face when he told him of his plan to frame him for the killings once his research was complete. Jerad was the perfect scapegoat.

When Luke got out and opened the trunk, he was happy to see the propofol he'd taken from his stepfather had done its job. Malorie was fast asleep.

CHAPTER THIRTY-EIGHT

Carolyn Delaney wore a monogrammed robe and what looked like matching pajamas underneath when she opened her front door. She didn't look any happier to see Stephenson than when he'd come to the university the previous day.

"I was just about to go to bed. What do you want?" she asked.

"I'd like to speak to your son, Luke. I have some questions for him about his missing classmate."

She ran her hand through her short dark hair and crossed her arms in front of her chest. "He's not here."

"Do you know where I might be able to find him?"

She stared at him for a moment before answering. "He's at the hospital. EBU Medical Center. He had a clinical rotation today in the ICU. You'll probably find my husband there as well."

Stephenson knew that Jerad had been suspended from both the hospital and university until he was either cleared of his charges or went to prison. "Why is Jerad at the hospital?" Stephenson asked.

She shrugged her shoulders. "Maybe you should ask him

while you're there." She started to close her front door. "Good night, Detective."

"Good night," Stephenson said as the door shut in his face.

Stephenson's phone rang when he got back to his car. It was Wade.

"Hey, Sergeant."

"I missed a couple calls from my niece, Malorie, and now I can't get a hold of her. She got an email from the same person who'd been emailing Lani from the shared computer at EBU Medical Center. I'm forwarding it to you. Also, she said she saw Jerad Delaney stealing drugs from the hospital tonight, but I don't know that it has any relevance to your investigation."

"I'm on my way to EBU Medical Center now." Stephenson filled his sergeant in on what they had learned about Luke.

"Good work. I'm already at the hospital. Elle's in labor."

"Oh, wow." Stephenson had almost forgotten that McKinnon was about to become a dad.

"I'll contact the hospital security and have them confirm if Luke's car is still here. I'll meet you at the main entrance when you get here."

"Are you sure? Don't you need to stay with Elle?"

"It's okay. The doctor said it's going to be awhile. Her sister is also here to keep her company."

"Okay. See you soon."

Just as he said, McKinnon was waiting for the detective at the main entrance of the hospital when Stephenson arrived.

"The hospital's security just confirmed to me that Luke's car is still parked in their parking garage. I'm having them check for Malorie's too. She said she was just leaving the hospital when she left the second voicemail, but she sounded scared. And now she's not answering."

"Luke's mother said he was working in the ICU."

"Let's go."

They followed the signs to the elevators and got off on the sixth floor. They went through the double doors leading to the ICU and stopped at the nurse's station. Stephenson showed his badge to a man wearing scrubs behind the desk.

"We're looking for Luke Paulson, a medical student who was working on this floor today," Stephenson said after introducing himself.

"Oh yeah, there was a medical student scheduled here today. I think his name was Luke. He called in sick this morning before I went home from the night shift. There weren't any other students on the unit."

Stephenson and McKinnon exchanged a look.

"Okay, thank you," Stephenson said. "Do you think he came here just to send Malorie that email?" he asked Wade as they walked out of the ICU. "Should we go wait by his car?"

"I'll call security and see if they can have someone watch it for us." Wade pulled out his phone. "Let's swing by the OR on our way out. I would guess that's where Malorie saw Jerad taking drugs. Maybe he stopped to see his stepdad before leaving."

He spoke with security as they walked to the elevators. He tucked his phone back into his pocket as the elevator doors opened. Stephenson hit the button for the third floor.

"Security found Malorie's car still parked here too," Wade said. "They said we might not be able to get into the OR at this time of night, so they'll have a security guard meet us outside the entrance."

They stepped out onto the third floor and turned left toward the OR. A security officer was waiting for them in front of double doors under a sign that read *After Hours Waiting Area*. The detectives quickly introduced themselves.

"Let's go this way." The officer pressed a button that opened the automatic doors.

A large man in scrubs lay on his back on the carpeted floor. The three men rushed toward the unmoving body. A surgical mask covered most of the man's face, but the skin that was visible had a grayish-blue hue. The man did not appear to be breathing.

Wade checked the man's neck for a pulse before he started CPR. Stephenson heard the security officer call the hospital operator.

"I have a code blue on the third floor in the OR after hours waiting area."

Stephenson noticed a needle and two empty syringes lay on the carpet next to the man's body. There was an obvious needle puncture mark in the man's left arm. The small amount of blood that seeped from the wound had not quite dried.

Stephenson knelt and undid the surgical mask that covered the man's mouth and nose. He immediately recognized the face of Jerad Delaney.

Less than a minute later, a small group of medical personnel carrying resuscitative equipment rushed into the room. They took over for Wade doing compressions, and the three men moved out of the team's way after Wade gave them a quick explanation of how they found the doctor.

"I'll draw up the narcan," one of the nurses said.

Stephenson and McKinnon stepped out into the hall to give them space to resuscitate Jerad. Two nurses rushed down the hall with an empty hospital bed for the anesthesiologist.

"A suicide attempt?" Stephenson asked Wade.

"It looks that way," Wade said. "And it might be more than an attempt."

The security officer was on his phone when he stepped out of the OR waiting room behind the detectives.

"My supervisor said Luke's car is still in the parking garage. He hasn't seen any sign of Luke," he said after ending the call.

At the end of the hall, the doors to the main OR opened. A short blonde nurse came through the doors, walking briskly in the direction of the after hours waiting area.

"Excuse me," Wade said as she approached them. Her name badge read *Natalie*. "I'm Sergeant McKinnon from Seattle Homicide. I'm looking for my niece, Malorie. She's a med student, and I believe she was here tonight in the OR. Do you know if she's still here?"

Natalie glanced at the activity inside the waiting area before returning his gaze. "Yeah, she was here. But she left over a half hour ago. She wasn't feeling well."

"Thank you," Wade said before she rushed into the waiting area.

CHAPTER THIRTY-NINE

Carolyn Delaney pressed her Hermès scarf against her neck as she stepped out of her Audi A4 into the cold night air. She could hardly contain her shock when the young, handsome detective had come to her home wanting to speak with Luke. First, he comes to the university and questions *her*. As if she could have had anything to do with the disappearance of Jerad's student. And now Luke.

The only guilty party in their family was her husband. But even he would never be capable of murder. Jerad was far too weak.

She'd directed the detective to the hospital, even though she knew Luke was likely home already from his shift. She'd tried calling Luke to warn him about Detective Stephenson, but he didn't answer. She didn't want her son to be bombarded by the detective like she had been when he'd questioned her at the university.

She walked through the quiet parking lot toward the lake and wondered what he wanted to speak to Luke about. Luke had nothing to do with the girl's disappearance. And her son had enough on his plate being in medical school with a stepfather who was just arrested for rape. Maybe *that* was what the detective wanted to ask him about.

Subconsciously, the corners of her mouth turned to a frown at the thought of her husband. She had almost reached the dock when she spotted Jerad's Mercedes parked at the edge of the parking lot.

She stopped and stared at his car. He would never visit Luke. They hated each other.

Had he come to threaten Luke in some way? What was he doing bothering her son?

There wasn't a day that went by she didn't regret her marriage to Jerad. If it weren't for her career, she would've divorced him long ago. But now things had changed.

After Jerad's second arrest for rape, she'd decided no one would blame her for leaving him. To the contrary, *staying* married to him might end her appointment as EBU President.

She cocked her head toward the sound of a boat engine cutting through the evening silence. She watched their yacht pull away from the dock. *What on earth was Jerad doing?* She watched the yacht pick up speed and head for the Fremont Cut.

She hurried down the dock and climbed onto Luke's rented houseboat. Maybe he knew what her husband was up to. She knocked for over a minute before giving up. She climbed back onto the dock, thinking she hadn't seen Luke's car in the parking lot. He must still be at the hospital.

She let out a sigh of exasperation as she headed back to her car. As she walked, she used the light from her phone to find the detective's business card in her purse.

CHAPTER FORTY

Stephenson's phone rang. He didn't recognize the number when he pulled it out of his suit pocket.

"Detective Stephenson."

"It's Carolyn. After you left my house, I drove down to Lake Union to see if Luke was at his houseboat. I was curious about why you wanted to speak to him. But, when I got there, I found Jerad's Mercedes in the parking lot and not Luke's Volvo. When I got close to the houseboat, I saw our yacht speed away from the dock.

"It seemed incredibly strange. Jerad hardly uses our boat in the summer, let alone on a cold autumn night. From what I could tell, it looked like the yacht was headed for the Fremont Cut. Since you were just at the house, I thought maybe you would want to know."

"How long ago did your boat leave?"

"Ten, maybe fifteen minutes ago. After it sped away, I went to the houseboat to check on Luke. No one answered when I knocked on the door."

"Can you give me a quick description of the yacht?"

"It's a fifty-foot motor cruiser. White and navy blue."

"Okay. Thanks for calling. And Carolyn?"

"Yes?"

"You should probably come to the hospital. When we went to question your husband, we found him unresponsive on the floor of the OR waiting area." Stephenson decided not to tell her the apparent reason for his collapse. "A medical team is working on him, but he didn't have a pulse when we found him."

He heard her draw in a sharp breath. "But I just saw his car parked on Lake Union."

Stephenson chose his words carefully. He didn't want to give her cause to warn her son they were on to him. "We think someone else may have been driving it."

"What? Who?"

"I'm sorry, but that's all I can tell you right now."

After he hung up, Stephenson told Wade what Carolyn had said.

"It must be Luke. I think he has Malorie. The email she received threatened her to back off. She said she was leaving the hospital when she left my voicemail. If she's on that boat, we have to get to her."

CHAPTER FORTY-ONE

Wade let Stephenson arrange for SWAT to get assembled and meet them at the Harbor Patrol Unit on Lake Union while he went to say good-bye to Elle in the Labor and Delivery Unit on the second floor. She smiled when he came through the door to her room. Kayla sat comfortably on the small couch next to Elle's bed.

He noticed Kayla was wearing hospital scrubs and must've come straight from her shift in the emergency room. Like Malorie, Kayla had also attended medical school at EBU. She'd recently finished her residency at Harborview and had just begun a fellowship in emergency medicine at EBU Medical Center.

Wade crossed the room and grabbed his wife's hand. "How are you doing? You look much more comfortable than when we first got here."

Elle nodded. "They just gave me an epidural. They said it might slow down the labor process, but I'm in a lot less pain."

"That's great."

"Did you find Malorie?" Elle asked.

"No. Um. I need to talk to you about that actually. Her car is here, but we can't find her. She told me she was leaving the hospital in the voicemail she left nearly an hour ago. We believe our prime suspect in Lani's disappearance was also here and may have taken Malorie captive on his parents' yacht."

"*What?*" Elle and Kayla said in unison.

"Stephenson is arranging for SWAT to meet us at Harbor Patrol so we can track down the boat and rescue Malorie if she's on it."

"Us?" Kayla asked.

Wade turned to Elle. "I know this is horrible timing but—"

"Go. Get to your niece. But come back here as soon as you can." She smiled. "I can't hold this baby in forever."

Wade leaned over and kissed her softly. "I love you," he whispered. He placed his hand on her belly. "And I promise I'll be back as soon as I can."

"Unbelievable," he heard his sister-in-law say as he stepped out of the room.

CHAPTER FORTY-TWO

Adams pulled into a parking spot near the quaint houseboat community on Lake Union that Stephenson had shown him earlier on his laptop. The area was a blend of industrial buildings, marinas, small waterfront parks, and clusters of houseboats. He stepped out of his car as an identical unmarked vehicle pulled up beside him.

"Thanks for coming, guys," Adams said as the two detectives got out of their car.

With Stephenson busy bringing in Luke for questioning, Adams had asked Tess and her partner, Detective Ben Suarez, to join him in searching the houseboat Luke currently leased. Tess had jumped at the chance to help with his investigation, especially since she'd been initially involved with Lani's case. Adams wondered if she was also looking for a distraction from her brother's upcoming murder trial. Whatever the reason, he appreciated the company. He'd learned in his many years being a homicide detective that it was always better to be overly prepared for the unknown.

They walked down the narrow dock lined by houseboats all in close proximity to each other. Adams could've thought of a lot more secluded places to keep someone hostage. After the three of them climbed aboard the back of the two-story vessel, Adams pounded his fist against the door.

"Seattle Police!"

After no response, Adams pulled his knee to his chest and kicked the door in. The sharp sound of the door getting ripped from its hinges before crashing to the floor would've surely woken the neighbors.

"Seattle Police!" Adams repeated as he stepped inside.

He held his gun out front with his right arm. His left arm was bent and crossed under the gun holding a flashlight. Tess and Ben did the same, following closely behind. They were met with silence in what appeared to be an empty houseboat.

"The room's clear," Adams announced after sweeping the main-level's kitchen and living room.

Tess pulled her sleeve over her hand before flicking on the light switch. The three detectives squinted as their eyes adjusted to the sudden brightness. The houseboat was clean and nicely decorated. It reminded Adams of something he'd seen on Airbnb.

"Seattle Police!" Adams called again.

There was no response.

Adams held up his gun and led the way up a narrow spiral staircase. The two other detectives' flashlights shone from behind him until he reached the top and turned on the hallway light. He crept slowly down the hall until he came upon a door.

He pivoted with his weapon outstretched before kicking the door open. He swung his firearm and flashlight across either side of the room.

The room felt a few degrees warmer than the rest of the

houseboat. A small desk with two computer screens was pushed against one wall. There was a twin mattress with a blanket and pillow on the floor next to the desk.

The far wall of the room was filled with medical equipment. There were two monitor screens mounted to the wall. They each appeared to display a heart rate and blood pressure along with a red waveform.

There were two IV poles with various fluids running through them on either side of waist-high medical stands. Adams stepped closer and noticed they looked to be equipped with internal temperature monitors and had plastic side rails around the top. He drew in a breath when he saw what was inside the fluid-filled bags atop each table.

"Oh my—" he heard Tess say from behind him.

One of the fetuses looked about two pounds bigger and more developed than the other. Adams guessed the larger one was Tina's and the smaller, less-developed one was Lani's.

"We should probably call the Neonatal Intensive Care Unit at EBU and find out how they want to transport them. They might want to send their own team instead of us calling 9-1-1," Tess said, staring at the tiny lifeforms. "I'll find the number."

"You think these are the babies of your victims?" Suarez asked.

Adams nodded. He couldn't tear his eyes from the two infants. The one he presumed was Lani's was the tiniest human he had ever seen. She had hardly any body fat, and her veins were visible beneath her translucent skin. It was incredible.

After a minute, he forced himself to step away and check the remainder of the houseboat. Suarez followed him out of the room. Adams moved to a door that was slightly ajar at the end of the hallway.

He stepped inside the small space, his gun and flashlight outstretched.

"It's clear," Adams said.

Ben turned on the lights. The room was about the same size as the last. It smelled strong of bleach.

There was a treadmill in one corner of the room and a hospital bed in the other. An IV pole stood next to the bed. The IV pump looked to be hospital-grade.

Adams stepped closer to the bed. The mattress was clean and bare. A total of four handcuffs were connected to the bedrails. The linoleum wood floor was spotless and had a light shine as if it had recently been mopped. The fresh smell of bleach and sparkling floors worried him the most out of everything in the room.

He turned to Ben.

"This doesn't look good," Suarez said.

Adams took a closer look at the bed. "No, it doesn't. We need to get CSI here ASAP to process everything."

"You want me to call them?" Suarez asked.

"Yes, thank you."

Ben pulled out his phone as Adams stepped out of the room. Tess met him in the hall before he returned to the room where they'd found the babies.

"The NICU is going to send a medical transport team over that is equipped to take these two little ones. They were pretty blown away by how we found them. I told them we were too."

Adams called McKinnon while they waited for the other teams to arrive. When he didn't answer, Adams tried Stephenson, but his phone also went to voicemail.

VIABLE HOSTAGE

"Stephenson, call me back as soon as you get this. You're not going to believe what we just found."

CHAPTER FORTY-THREE

Stephenson hung up with the Ballard Locks operator when Wade met him at the entrance to the hospital.

"SWAT should be ready to go at the Harbor Patrol Unit in twenty minutes," Stephenson said as they speed-walked to his car. "I just got off the phone with the operator at the Ballard Locks. I told him not to let any boats through, but he said he'd just opened the locks for a yacht that matches the description of the Delaneys' boat. The boat's already taken off."

"We better hurry then," Wade said as he clicked in his seatbelt.

Stephenson turned on his lights and siren as he peeled out of the hospital parking lot in his unmarked car.

Nineteen minutes later, Stephenson and Wade sat side by side on the Harbor Patrol motor craft as it pulled away from the dock on Lake Union. They sped across the lake and took a sharp turn onto the Fremont Cut that would lead them out to the Sound.

Stephenson inadvertently leaned into his sergeant as they made the corner. Wade had barely spoken a word since they left the hospital. Stephenson knew he was probably grappling with the reality that if his niece had been taken captive on Luke's boat, she might already be dead. The fact that Luke was taking Malorie to the same waters where he had presumably disposed of Tina's body did not favor Malorie being alive.

Stephenson looked across at the four SWAT members who had joined them. He'd heard stories about McKinnon's partner, Cody, who'd been shot and killed when they'd failed to take SWAT with them on an arrest several years back.

Stephenson checked his phone and saw that he'd missed a call from Adams. He dialed his partner.

"Hey, you're not going to believe what we found at the houseboat. Where are you?"

Stephenson could barely hear his partner over the patrol boat engine. He pressed his finger against his other ear.

"We're with harbor patrol," Stephenson yelled. "We think Luke's taken Malorie captive on his parents' yacht."

"Wade's niece?"

"Yeah. What'd you find at the houseboat?"

"There's evidence Luke was holding someone here, probably both Tina and Lani. We also found two more victims, but they're alive."

"Two more women?"

"Not quite," Adams said. "We believe they are Tina and Lani's babies."

"And they're *alive*?" Stephenson said.

"Yes. I'll tell you more when I see you."

After hanging up, Stephenson leaned over to Wade and reiterated what Adams had said. His sergeant raised his eyebrows when Stephenson told him about the babies.

"I didn't think either of them were that far along," Wade

said.

Stephenson shrugged his shoulders. "They weren't. But Adams said they were alive. He said he'll tell me more in person."

"They didn't find Lani?"

Stephenson shook his head. What Adams had found likely confirmed Luke was their killer, which was not good news if Malorie was captive on his yacht.

The patrol boat's large, bright beams flooded the dark canal with light. They cruised past the large buildings that made up part of the EBU campus. The other side of the canal was mostly residential. Stephenson found it strange seeing the well-kept waterfront homes, quiet and peaceful, when they were about to be faced with the possible deaths of Wade's niece and Lani Wu.

The gates were immediately opened for them when they reached the locks. A lockwall attendant was waiting to tie up their boat to the pier after they entered. Fifteen minutes later, the water inside the lock had drained to sea level. After the gate was opened, they sped through the bay and entered the Sound.

Stephenson heard one of the SWAT detectives get a call on his radio. He acknowledged the message and got up to speak to the patrol boat captain. Before returning to his seat, the SWAT detective stepped across the boat and spoke into Wade's ear. Wade turned to Stephenson as the SWAT detective took a seat across from them.

"Our helicopter has tracked Luke's boat about a mile north of Bainbridge Island. They made a quick overpass so they don't spook him. They're going to wait for us to get a little closer to announce their presence. Luke cruised a little farther past the island before turning around. He hasn't come to a stop but he's slowed down."

Probably looking for a good spot to dump a body, Stephenson thought to himself. He didn't have to say it out loud; he knew Wade was thinking the same thing.

CHAPTER FORTY-FOUR

The floor moved under Malorie when she awoke. She was groggy. She wanted nothing more than to go back to sleep. She closed her eyelids and remembered running from Luke. Malorie lifted her heavy head from the floor only to have it come up and smack her in the temple. The floor continued to roll as she looked around the dark surroundings.

Her eyes adjusted to the dark and she saw that she was in someone's living room. She heard the loud roar of an engine and knew she must be on a boat. *Luke's boat.*

She struggled to get up. Her wrists were bound together behind her back. Her body felt incredibly weak. There was a fogginess in her head that wouldn't clear. She got to her knees but failed to keep her balance when the vessel rolled. She landed on her side. She inadvertently flipped onto her back before she came to a stop against the base of a couch.

A large, heavy tarp rolled into her, sandwiching Malorie between its dead weight and the built-in sofa. Malorie tried to shove the tarp away from her, but it didn't move easily.

She nearly jumped onto the couch when she felt the firm limbs of the lifeless body. A cold, stiff hand slipped out from the plastic onto the thin carpet.

Malorie sat up despite the spinning in her head. She willed her eyes to focus on who was beneath the tarp. Light from the full moon shone onto the floor through the yacht's window. It only took her a moment to know beyond a doubt it was Lani. Tears streamed down Malorie's face as she saw Lani's long dark hair, beautiful brown eyes now stripped of life, and her ridiculously long false lashes. She lowered her head over her friend's face.

"Oh, Lani," she cried. "I'm so sorry. I'm so sorry I was too late."

Malorie rested her forehead against her beautiful friend's chest through the thick plastic. Through her sobs, she was unaware the boat had come to a stop.

"I picked you for more of a light-weight," Luke's voice came from the corner of the room.

Malorie saw his tall, lean outline in the doorway leading to the outer deck. She wanted to squeeze Lani's hand, even though she knew her friend could no longer feel her touch.

"I guess I should've given you more propofol."

"Why did you do this to her?" Malorie said through her sobs.

Luke let out an exaggerated sigh. "It was for a greater good. But I don't expect you to understand."

Malorie sat back against the couch as the psychopath stepped toward them. Luke's sneakers were only inches from Lani's head when he came to a stop. Malorie looked up at him, disgusted at herself for liking him when he had been the one who'd taken Lani all along.

Luke clapped his gloved hands together. "Well, who wants to go first?"

Although Malorie couldn't see well enough in the dark, she sensed he was smiling.

VIABLE HOSTAGE

"No volunteers? Okay, I'll choose."

CHAPTER FORTY-FIVE

"There it is." Wade stood from his seat at the sight of Luke's parents' yacht, which appeared to be idling in the distance.

Stephenson stood up next to him as they rapidly approached the cruiser. All four SWAT detectives stood on the side of the boat with their guns drawn. With the help of the spotlight from the helicopter, Wade could make out a tall man standing at the rear of the yacht. As they sped closer, Wade saw Luke was holding a much shorter woman in front of himself, using her as a human shield against the weapons aimed at him from the helicopter and incoming boat. *Malorie*. Wade moved to the front of the boat as their captain came over the intercom.

"Turn off your motor and place your hands atop your head," the officer's voice resounded across the water. "This is Seattle Police."

Luke ignored both of the captain's orders. Keeping Malorie pressed tight against his chest, Luke stepped backward on the yacht, seeming to move closer to the helm. The patrol boat slowed as they neared Luke's vessel. They were within thirty feet of Luke's boat, and Wade saw his niece's arms appeared to be bound behind her back. Luke reached the other side of the boat, but, instead of turning off the engine, he pivoted.

Luke scooped up Malorie by placing an arm under her knees. He swung her body over the side of his boat and Malorie disappeared over the edge. Wade wanted to jump in after her, but they weren't close enough.

Luke turned for the yacht's helm. Without his human shield, gunfire from the SWAT detectives exploded in his direction. Luke fell against the side of the boat from the impact of a bullet in his arm. He crouched and tucked into the yacht's enclosed helm. The yacht's engine roared to life as the harbor patrol boat closed in on him. The SWAT detectives fired their weapons as Luke's boat sped away.

With Malorie in the water, the patrol boat continued to slow despite Luke's attempt to escape. Wade leaned over the side, searching the dark water for his niece under the helicopter's spot light. The seconds felt like hours until he spotted movement in the choppy sea.

Wade pointed at the water. "She's there! I see her!"

Without hesitation, Wade unzipped his bulletproof vest and dove into the frigid ocean. He took swift strokes toward his niece, despite the drag from his suit and the shock of the cold. Malorie's movements were growing slower, as she struggled to stay on the surface with her wrists bound. She sank beneath the waves just before Wade reached her.

Wade dove beneath the spot where she'd disappeared. He felt the floating fabric of her sweatshirt and wrapped his arm around her waist. He kicked to the surface. Wade drew in as big a breath as his lungs would allow in the cold water. Malorie coughed before inhaling a large gulp of air.

The patrol boat pulled up beside them and threw them a life ring. Still holding his niece, Wade looped his arm around it. Malorie let out a series of hard coughs as they were assisted onto the boat. Blankets were draped around each of them.

"Did we lose him?" Wade asked Stephenson.

Stephenson nodded. "The captain just radioed the helicopter pilot to continue its pursuit. It looks like Luke turned off the yacht's lights." Stephenson turned to the harbor patrol officer. "We need something to cut the tape around her wrists."

The officer handed him a knife. Malorie turned to allow Stephenson to remove the tape from her wrists. She huddled close to her uncle on the bench as they shivered side by side.

The captain opened the door from inside the helm. "They've spotted him. He's headed for the passage between the northwest side of Bainbridge and the mainland. I need everyone to take a seat."

The patrol boat sped ahead seconds after the captain closed the door.

Stephenson sat next to Wade. "Hold on," Stephenson said to Malorie. "We've still got to stop Luke."

The three of them leaned to the right as the patrol boat turned around and took off in the direction of Luke's yacht. Wade spotted the helicopter in the distance, shining its light on Luke's cruiser for them to follow.

Malorie hunched closer to her uncle, trying to escape the cold wind as the patrol boat picked up speed. The boat flew past the northern end of the island. They sped across the Sound, closing the space between them and Luke's yacht. When they drew close to his boat, the captain made a sharp left. They continued north until they were cruising right beside Luke's yacht.

Stephenson had been right. The yacht's lights were off. It would've been impossible to see without the spotlight from the helicopter above.

The SWAT detectives were back in position, weapons drawn. Luke crouched low in the enclosed helm, which protected him from any incoming gunfire.

His yacht remained in the center of the bright beam shining from the helicopter.

"Stop your boat and turn off your engine," their captain's voice boomed through the boat's intercom. "Then place your hands above your head!"

Luke's yacht continued to speed along beside them. The SWAT detectives fired a round in his direction. Luke glanced at their boat in response to the incoming gunfire. He sank lower into the enclosed helm.

Wade watched Stephenson step across the boat as it pulled closer to Luke's yacht. The two vessels were moving at practically the same speed. Wade realized what the young detective was about to do a moment before Stephenson climbed onto the side of their boat and launched himself across the water onto Luke's yacht.

Wade crossed to where Stephenson had jumped. "Hold your fire!" he said to the SWAT detectives.

Although Stephenson had managed to get himself onto Luke's yacht, he hadn't landed on his feet. The yacht took a sharp right as Stephenson struggled to stand. Luke's vessel veered away from the patrol boat, and Stephenson moved to his hands and knees. He'd started to stand when Luke left the wheel and rushed toward him.

Wade watched Stephenson reach for his gun, but it was too late. Luke lunged toward Stephenson, swinging a long fillet knife at the detective. Stephenson's body kept the

VIABLE HOSTAGE

SWAT detectives from having a clear shot at Luke, especially with the movement of the boats.

Wade gripped the edge of the patrol boat as it leaned into a hard turn toward Luke's yacht. As they got closer, Wade saw Luke's blade come within inches of Stephenson's throat. Stephenson pulled his hand away from his holstered weapon and wrapped both hands around Luke's wrist. Stephenson forced Luke backward and slammed Luke's hand against the side of the doorway to the enclosed helm. Luke appeared to maintain a hold on the knife as the two men disappeared inside the boat.

The patrol boat moved into position next to Luke's yacht, matching the larger boat's speed. Wade swore before stepping onto the side of the boat and jumping across. He landed hard, just inside Luke's boat. He fell to his side on the yacht's deck and was reminded that he wasn't as young as he used to be. The yacht's interior cabin was dark. Wade noticed a large, bloodied tarp rolled into a ball in the corner of the rear deck.

He started to get to his feet when the boat dipped from a large swell. A shot rang out from inside the cabin as Wade fell to his knees. Luke appeared in the cabin doorway, his handgun aimed at Wade's chest. Wade unholstered his weapon at the same time as two more shots rang out, one after the other. He watched Luke's body jerk in response to the bullets in his back before he collapsed forward onto the deck. Luke hit the hull with a thud. His gun fell away from his grip and slid to the rear of the boat.

Wade slowly lowered his weapon. He saw movement inside the cabin seconds before the young detective appeared in the doorway over Luke's body. Stephenson kept his gun aimed at Luke's torso, but Luke remained still.

"You hurt?" Wade asked.

"I'm fine," he said, dropping his gun to his side.

Wade turned and motioned to the helicopter and patrol boat that they were okay before he went to the helm. Wade put the yacht in neutral while Stephenson checked Luke's carotid artery for a pulse. Once the boat had stopped, the SWAT detectives came aboard.

"There's no pulse," Stephenson told them before starting CPR.

"We've just radioed Seattle Fire, and they're sending out Marine One, the Fire Rescue Boat they had on stand-by," one of the SWAT detectives said.

The SWAT detective moved toward the helm while another kneeled next to Stephenson, ready to take over compressions if he got tired.

"Go be with your niece," the SWAT detective told Wade. "I'll drive us back, and we'll meet the fireboat halfway."

"All right, thank you." Wade stepped aside, allowing the detective to take his place.

Wade moved past Stephenson and could hear him counting aloud as he continued CPR on Luke. He'd have to thank him later for saving his life. Wade wasted no time in climbing back onto the Harbor Patrol Unit so they could get Luke to the medic unit as quickly as possible. Wade wrapped his arm around his niece's blanketed shoulders as they rode back to the city. Malorie hunkered against him as the cold, damp wind blew through her wet hair. Between sobs, she told him about Lani, how Luke had tossed her dead body overboard about ten minutes before they arrived. It explained the tarp he'd seen on the rear of the boat.

The helicopter was continuing to search the waters for

her, and they had already called the Coast Guard to assist in their search.

"Thanks for saving me," she said.

He kissed the top of her head. "That's what uncles are for. I'm sorry we weren't able to save your friend."

Wade could see his niece was overcome with emotion. A moment passed before she responded. "Me too. But I know you did everything you could." She turned to face him as they approached the lights from the city. "Elle hasn't gone into labor yet?"

"She's actually at EBU Medical Center in labor right now. Hopefully, she still is."

Malorie leaned her head back against her uncle's shoulder. Despite the crushing loss of her best friend, she smiled. "You're going to make a great dad."

CHAPTER FORTY-SIX

Wade jogged down the corridor of the Labor and Delivery Unit at EBU. His wet dress shoes made an audible squish with each step. He'd tried calling both Elle and Kayla using Stephenson's phone but neither had answered his calls.

He'd ridden to the hospital in the ambulance with Malorie after they'd been dropped off at a downtown pier. One of the firemen had given Wade a Seattle Fire Department t-shirt and sweatpants they kept in the ambulance. Wade had changed in a hospital bathroom. His wet suit was rolled into a ball under his arm.

Wade heard the wail of a newborn as he neared Elle's hospital room. He picked up his pace. Wade swung open the door as the doctor placed his infant son on a warmer adjacent to Elle's bed. Wade beamed at his wife, who still looked incredibly beautiful after childbirth. He moved toward the table, admiring his child as the nurse dried him off.

"Congratulations, Dad," the nurse said.

Kayla took a photo with her phone from the other side of the warmer as Wade reached for his son's tiny hand. His son continued to wail as the nurse placed a hat on his head and hospital bands around his wrist and ankle.

"Thank you."

"He's got good lungs," Kayla said with a smile. "And he looks just like you," she added.

After placing a diaper on him, the nurse wrapped him in a blanket and handed Wade his son. "You can take him to his mom now."

"Does he have a name?" the nurse asked as Wade placed him in Elle's arms.

"Cody," Wade said.

Kayla took more photos as Wade and Elle took in their child's beauty for the first time. Wade kissed Elle on the forehead.

"I'm sorry I missed his birth."

"It's okay. I'm glad you're here now. Plus, Kayla was probably better support during the labor process than you anyway," she teased.

"Thanks for filling in for me," Wade said to his sister-in-law.

"No problem, Sergeant."

Kayla smiled, and Wade accepted her lighthearted reference to his rank as a step in the right direction.

"Did you find Malorie?" Elle asked.

"Yes. She's okay. She's downstairs being treated for hypothermia and a mild concussion, but she's going to be fine." Wade refrained from telling her about Lani. He'd wait until she asked.

"Thank God."

Cody had stopped crying. His mouth followed Elle's finger as she stroked the side of his face.

"That's called rooting," her nurse said. "That's good. It means he's hungry."

VIABLE HOSTAGE

"Isn't he perfect?" Elle said to Wade.

Tears filled Wade's eyes as all of the emotions from that day began to surface. "Yes. He is."

Two hours later, Wade and Elle were alone in their room with Cody when there was a knock at their door.

"Come in," Wade said.

Malorie slowly stepped inside. She wore a hospital gown, robe, and slippers.

"I'm here to meet my little cousin," she said.

"We're so glad you're okay," Elle said.

Malorie moved to Elle's bed and the two women exchanged a hug. "Thank you."

Wade wheeled Cody's bassinet next to Malorie. Cody was sleeping peacefully, snugly wrapped in a hospital blanket with a tan beanie atop his head.

"He's so cute," Malorie said.

"Do you want to hold him?" Wade asked.

"I don't want to wake him," she said.

"You won't. It's fine."

Malorie sat in the chair next to Elle's bed as Wade carefully placed Cody in her lap. "Hey little buddy," she whispered. "I'm your favorite cousin."

"You don't have to stay in the hospital overnight?" Wade asked.

"No. They discharged me from the emergency room. I have a mild concussion, and they were able to get my body temperature up pretty quickly since I wasn't in the water that long."

"That's good," Wade said.

Malorie held Cody for a little while longer before placing

him back in his crib. "I should let you two get some rest."

"You too," Wade said as he walked her to the door.

"Thanks for coming up to see us," Elle said.

"Do you have a ride home?" Wade asked.

"Yeah. Lani's parents."

It hadn't taken Elle long to ask about Lani, and Wade was glad now that he'd told her. So far, the Coast Guard hadn't found her body. They hadn't called off the search yet, but if they didn't find her soon, Wade knew they would probably suspend their search until the morning.

"I'm so sorry about your friend," Elle said.

Wade put his hand on his niece's shoulder. "Me too."

"Thank you. I just hope her baby survives."

Wade wasn't sure what the odds were, but from what he knew, Lani's baby was only on the brink of viability—if that.

Stephenson had called Wade after he took a statement from Malorie in the ER and had told her what Adams had found when he searched Luke's houseboat. A patrol unit had been waiting to take Stephenson to the hospital after they met up with the Fire Rescue Boat. After interviewing Malorie, he'd learned that Luke had been pronounced dead on arrival when the medics brought him to the ER.

When he'd informed Carolyn Delaney of her son's death, Stephenson had also learned that Jerad Delaney had been pronounced dead shortly after he and Wade had left the hospital. It appeared that he'd injected himself with enough propofol and fentanyl to kill a horse.

Wade's heart went out to Carolyn for the devastating loss of her son and husband in one night. For the rest of the world, however, their deaths might've been a blessing. Wade hugged Malorie before she left, thankful she was alive.

He'd seen a lot of darkness in his life. He was glad he'd

been able to overcome some of his own demons so he could witness the birth of his child and be a good influence on his niece, who was just starting life as an adult. After holding his infant son in his arms, Wade's fears about not being a good father faded away. He knew, without a shadow of a doubt, that he would do anything for Cody. He might not be perfect, but he would make sure he was the best father to his son that he knew how to be.

CHAPTER FORTY-SEVEN

Malorie met Lani's parents at the entrance to the Neonatal Intensive Care Unit.

Lani's mother pulled her into a tight embrace. "Thank you for doing your best to find her," Lani's mother said. "We should've believed you when you knew something was wrong." She wiped a tear from her eye. "You were always such a good friend to our daughter."

Malorie nodded, unable to speak from the emotions that choked out her voice.

The double doors to the NICU swung open. A nurse in navy blue scrubs appeared in the doorway. "You can come through now," she said.

Malorie followed Lani's parents through the quiet hallway. Sliding glass doors leading to private rooms lined the hall on one side. They turned a corner and the nurse instructed them to scrub their hands at the sink for two minutes before entering Lani's baby's room. As the three of them scrubbed, the nurse explained that premature babies were at high risk of developing infections due to their premature immune system and skin integrity.

"Is she going to live?" Malorie asked the nurse.

"It's too soon to say for certain, but she's stable. Based on her development, she appears to be between twenty-three and twenty-four weeks gestation. We've had babies survive in our unit from that age before. She's got a long road ahead, but so far she's doing well. It's possible the way she was kept in an artificial uterine environment saved her life. But only time will tell."

The nurse instructed them to keep their voices down before entering the room. Malorie let out an audible gasp when she saw Lani's baby girl lying in the humidified isolette. She was so tiny. The whiteboard on the wall said she weighed only one pound.

Malorie moved closer. Knowing Lani's parents were both doctors and Malorie a medical student, the nurse gave only a brief explanation of the various medical equipment and asked if they had any questions.

"No, thank you," Lani's father said.

"I'll be right outside if you need me," she said before stepping out of the room.

Tears streamed down Lani's father's face as he wrapped his arm around his wife. Malorie stood on the opposite side of the isolette. Lani's baby had IVs that fed through her umbilical cord and a breathing tube that looked smaller than a straw. Although her eyes were fused, they were covered with tiny fabric shades to protect her from the phototherapy light shining through the top of her isolette.

She wore only a tiny diaper and had hardly any body fat. Malorie could see her chest move with every heartbeat. She knew from med school that it was referred to as an active precordium.

They watched her in silence for ten minutes longer before Lani's parents backed away from the isolette.

VIABLE HOSTAGE

"We'd better get you home," Lani's father said.

"Okay." Malorie turned and took one last look at Lani's tiny little girl before she followed them out of the room.

She'd called her parents while she was being treated in the ER, and they were on their way, driving up from Portland, after hearing all that had happened.

"We'll have to do a paternity test to find out who the father is, although we're pretty sure it's Dante," Lani's mother told her after they exited the unit. "But we're going to see if we can get full custody."

"I'd be happy to help out with her if you do," Malorie said.

"I know." Lani's mother grabbed Malorie by the hand. "But right now she needs our prayers more than anything."

"If she's anything like her mother," Malorie said, "She's got a fighting chance."

WANT MORE?

Get your FREE bonus content and new release updates at
AUDREYJCOLE.COM/sign-up

Detectives Blake Stephenson and Tess Richards will return in the next Emerald City Thriller

EMERALD CITY THRILLERS BY AUDREY J. COLE

THE RECIPIENT

INSPIRED BY MURDER

THE SUMMER NANNY

VIABLE HOSTAGE

ABOUT THE AUTHOR

Audrey J. Cole is a registered nurse and a writer of thrillers set in Seattle. After living in Australia for the last five years, Audrey has returned to the Pacific Northwest where she resides with her husband and two children.

Connect with Audrey:
facebook.com/AudreyJCole
bookbub.com/authors/Audrey-J-Cole
instagram.com/AudreyJCole/

You can also visit her website:
www.AUDREYJCOLE.com

Made in the USA
Middletown, DE
04 May 2025